The Last Rose

Stories of family and friendship

WENDY CLARKE

For permission requests, email:
editor@cobblestonewalkpublishing.co.uk

Published by Cobblestone Walk Publishing

First published 2015

Author: Wendy Clarke

http://wendyswritingnow.blogspot.co.uk

ISBN-13: 978-1508501497
ISBN-10: 1508501491

'The Last Rose' is a collection of thirteen stories of family and friendship by Wendy Clarke, a regular writer of fiction for national magazines.

All of these stories have previously been published in either 'The People's Friend', 'Take a Break Fiction Feast' or 'Woman's Weekly'. If you like stories with emotional depth and a satisfying ending, then this collection is for you.

'Wendy Clarke has become one of The People's Friend's most valued writers, offering our readers a range of themes and a level of emotional satisfaction that is rare in the short story format.'

Shirley Blair

Commissioning Fiction Editor for 'The People's Friend'

CONTENTS

SAYING GOODBYE TO SUMMER

It was seven minutes past ten when Vanessa said goodbye to Summer; she knew this because the clock on the kitchen wall had told her so. Summer was off to Manchester University in Martin's Renault – so full of boxes of kitchen implements, holdalls of clothes, duvets and potted plants that he was unable to use the rear view mirror.

Summer had laughed and swung her mother around the kitchen that morning: the future ahead of her, the world her oyster, the sky the limit – clichés written for that moment, Vanessa thought. Without a backward glance and with no uncertainty in her young mind, Summer had left her a blown kiss and a heart full of memories. Vanessa knew that this was as it should be.

A week later, she and Martin had not yet had a phone call. They were standing in the doorway to Summer's room. This was where Summer had played, slept, dressed up in fairy wings and lined up her dolls for their fashion parades. It was the room where she had written secrets in her diary and where she and her friends had made plans to marry Robbie Williams. Today was the day that they had chosen to clear the room.

'I don't know why but it seems different this time, doesn't it?' Vanessa ran a finger along the spines of the books on the shelf. Harry Potter squashed between Little Women and Sophie's Snail. 'I can't believe how the time has flown.'

Martin studied the pastel pink walls with their border of purple flowers. 'How about blue this time?'

She noticed how he didn't answer her question.

'I think blue would be nice.'

When people asked her how she could bear to clear out her child's room so soon, she would simply smile and turn away.

Summer's room would be easy. She had always been a tidy child and together they had regularly sorted out her clothes and old toys to be taken to the charity shop. She had only ever kept what was special to her. What little she had left behind would be quickly sorted.

'Shall we box what's left and put it in the spare room for when she comes home for holidays?'

It had been a different story when Tim had left. When they had said goodbye to him, it was as if he had left his whole life behind in his room. They had found boxes of rocks and minerals that had been collecting dust under the bed and Pokemon cards that had fought for their share of the chest of drawers along with jam jars of foreign coins and a tank of stick insects. It had taken the best part of a week to clear it.

2

'She hasn't called yet. I would have thought she would have by now.' Martin was as keen as Vanessa was for the phone to ring. It was always the same – excitement mixed with a little expectation.

'What do you think she'll say?'

'Probably that she'll visit in a couple of weeks – to make sure that everything's all right. I'm sure she'll ring soon. Do you need any more boxes? I'll go and get some out of the garage.'

Vanessa parted the net curtains and looked at the view that her children had looked out at over the years – to the right, the small grassy area, with the small playground, where Darren had broken his arm after jumping off the swing before it had stopped; to the left, the path that led between the row of bungalows to the shingle beach where Leanne had first learned to paddle a canoe.

The day Summer had left, Elaine from over the road had asked Vanessa how she was feeling. 'It's hard when they go isn't it?'

It was difficult for Vanessa to explain, in a way that people would understand, that instead of feeling upset, her heart nearly burst with pride each time she said goodbye to one of her children – knowing that her job was done and that she had helped to guide them along the stony path to adulthood.

She started to strip the bed. As she lifted the pillow, ready to plump it, she noticed a folded piece of paper. 'Vanessa' was written on the front. She thought about calling for Martin but something stopped her – she wanted to keep the moment to herself. Slowly she opened the note.

How did I know that you would be making my bed! I don't know when you'll find this but I bet it will be before I get round to ringing. You know I've always been useless at communication – isn't that what you said that time I forgot to tell you I was staying over at Lara's and you called all my friends at midnight? Just think, now you can sing as loud as you like to Michael Bouble, without having to hear me groan. And you can go on that trip to Canterbury you keep talking about without worrying about what I'm getting up to (we never did manage to get rid of that red wine stain did we!) Anyway, I just wanted to say thank you both for everything you've done for me. I'll try and remember to eat fruit now and again and empty the rubbish bin! See you in reading week.

Summer x

Vanessa pushed the note into her pocket and picked up a photograph that had been standing on Summer's bedside table. It had been taken when she was still at primary school. She handed it to Martin as he came up the stairs.

'Another to add to the collection,' she said. On the landing, framed prints of their children smiled down at them.

She had said goodbye to many children over the decades: to Tim who had left to study geology at Exeter University; to Leanne who had moved just two streets away with her boyfriend and her baby; to Darren who had gone into the fire service and Joe who had moved to a special residential school. She had said goodbye to others too – the ones who had run away or moved back to their mothers and those children who had stayed just a week or a day or even just a night. Moments of childhood captured in the blink of a camera's shutter.

The phone rang, making them both jump and Martin ran to their bedroom to answer it. As she listened to his voice rise and fall, she found that her fingers were crossed behind her back.

'That was the social worker.' There was a huge grin on Martin's face. 'She's going to bring Carl over to see us next Tuesday. She thinks that he'll be with us for a couple of months but you never know – that's what they said about Summer. His current foster carer is finding it difficult to cope with him at the moment. It's very sad.'

'I know.' Vanessa put her arms around her husband. 'Look, we'll do our best for him – like we always do and hope that it works out.'

Martin held Summer's photograph up to a space on the wall beside Tim's. 'Here I think.' He turned to Vanessa. 'We've done a good job, haven't we?'

Vanessa smiled and squeezed his shoulder. 'We've done more than that.' Handing him Summer's letter, she watched as Martin scanned the loopy writing, a smile hovering on his lips.

'So, she's going to eat some vegetables, is she? That's something,' he said, sitting down on the top step. 'Do you remember that time in France when all she would eat was snails and chips?'

'How could I forget,' Vanessa replied. She joined him on the step, smiling at the memory. So many wonderful memories, of all their foster children stacked one upon the other like an album.

That night as she and Martin lay in bed, Vanessa was aware of how quiet the house seemed and she thought how nice it would be to hear a child's voice again. A smile played on her lips as she drifted off to sleep – she was remembering the P.S. at the bottom of Summer's letter.

Don't forget – It's not goodbye it's just au revoir!

LOOK AT ME

Natalie has had a bad day at school. I can tell by the way she is sitting, hunched over her drawing book, her face screwed up in concentration. As I walk round behind her, the back door, which I had left open, slams and my daughter jumps. She stares at the door. She doesn't like loud noises, or bright lights or anything that feels funny in her mouth. You see, my six-year-old daughter has Aspergers.

'Nat?'

She looks back down at the page. I see that it is covered in pencil marks. She has drawn squares and rectangles, some big and some small. The lines are thick and heavy, for she finds holding the pencil difficult, but she concentrates on them as if they were a work of art – and of course they are, to me.

'There are twelve squares and nine rectangles,' she says, drawing another, 'and now there are thirteen squares and nine rectangles.'

This is what Natalie does when something is troubling her: she draws and she counts. Mrs Pollard, her teacher, said that her numeracy skills are among the best in the class. I can't tell you how pleased that made me feel... and how proud.

I knew that Natalie was different early in her little life. When she cried, and I picked her up and held her close to my chest, my rocking only made her worse and it was only when I placed her in her cot that she would settle. Later, I began to notice that when my friends' babies started to smile at their mothers, Natalie's face would remain passive if I played peek-a-boo or sang to her.

At first, I put it down to the fact that, along with new motherhood, I was struggling to keep my marriage together. We had married too young; I see that now and the people we were to become were not the same as those we had been when Dan put the simple diamond ring on my finger. He had tried, or so he said, but fatherhood had not come naturally to him and two years after our little daughter was born, we were divorced.

'Want to tell me what's up, Natalie?'

My little girl tilts her head towards the ceiling, her brown eyes searching the Artex for whatever mysteries might be there. I berate myself for being so stupid: sometimes it's as if six years with Natalie has taught me nothing.

'I meant what's wrong, Natalie. Did something happen at school that,' I choose the words more carefully, 'you didn't like?'

She turns her head to me but her eyes don't meet mine, instead fixing on the row of cookery books on the kitchen counter behind me.

'Mrs Pollard wasn't there today.'

'Oh, dear,' I say. 'Was she feeling bad?'

Natalie shakes her little head. 'Mrs Pollard would never do anything bad. She says that if you are bad you won't get a sticker on the chart and Mrs Pollard doesn't have a chart.'

'What I meant to say is, was Mrs Pollard unwell?'

'Yes. She has the flu. Mrs James came in and said we were to have another teacher but I didn't want another teacher.' I am about to speak but she continues. 'Mrs James took me out of the class and I went in with Mrs Collins' class because I know her but then they did writing when we should have been doing sums and I screamed.'

Natalie's face shows no emotion as she says this and I wonder what she is feeling. I am rather surprised that the school didn't ring me up but then they are used to Natalie's ways and it would seem that they managed.

'You shouldn't have screamed at Mrs Collins, Natalie. You like her.'

Natalie pushes her glasses up her nose. 'Yes, but Mrs Collins said that it was English when it should have been sums.'

Knowing that it will be pointless to question her further, I suggest an outing. The weather has been good despite it being October and I know something that will make Natalie's day a little better.

'Shall we go and see Misty?'

Natalie finishes the square she is drawing and then puts down the pencil. 'Yes.'

She allows me to lift her off the stool but I don't help her with her coat, as she likes to put it on herself.

'Now the scarf.' The scarf is one that my mother knitted and Natalie likes to wear it whatever the weather. 'Now the gloves.'

When she is ready, we let ourselves out of the back door. There are paving stones curving around the edge of the lawn, making a path to the back gate, but Natalie prefers to walk the straight line across the grass. We let ourselves out into the lane and stop to look for traffic.

'To make it safe to cross the road, use ears as well as eyes. Never run but take good care and you'll be very wise.'

Even though there is no traffic, I know better than to take Natalie's hand and lead her across the farm track until she has recited the rhyme I taught her. We go through this ritual every time we cross a road and, as there are four between our house and the school, I have to make sure that we leave in good time.

'Now we can cross, Mum.'

The sun is going down, taking its warmth with it. I see Natalie shiver but resist putting my arm around her little shoulders.

'There he is!' Natalie runs along the hedgerow to the five-barred gate and just as she says, there is Misty. His head leans over the top bar of the gate and he flicks it from side to side to rid himself of the flies that rise then settle.

Natalie stands on tiptoe and holds out her hand; I see she has a half-eaten apple in it. She offers it to him and, as he takes it, she giggles as his leathery lips tickle her skin. I stand back and watch, a smile on my face. It's a sound I rarely hear and it is beautiful.

She climbs up onto the rusty bar of the gate and, lifting her hand, strokes the side of his face then leans her head towards him. Her face softens and she smiles. I hear her murmuring to the grey horse and wonder what she is saying. I hear the words *Mrs Pollard* and *sums* and guess that she is telling him about her day.

Misty snorts, sending a plume of breath into the evening air and Natalie strokes his nose. 'I love you Misty,' she says and my heart clenches; it is something she has never said to me.

'Come on, love. Let's go back and I'll make you cocoa before bed.' Natalie always has cocoa. 'I know today wasn't the best but tomorrow is another day.'

Natalie gives Misty a last pat and steps down from the gate.

'Obviously it is,' she says.

She lets me take her hand, although I know she'd rather I didn't, and we leave Misty's field. As we do, I notice that we are not alone. At the side of the field near the gate that leads to a large Elizabethan farmhouse, a man leans against a quad bike. He must have been there a while, as I hadn't heard the sound of the engine. I have seen him before, on other occasions, striding across the field in his muddy wellingtons or driving a tractor along the lane.

When he sees us looking, he raises a hand in greeting and calls out something. I hope he won't come over, as Natalie isn't keen on strangers so I pretend not to see and walk back down the lane, remembering to salute the magpie that we see so as not to upset Natalie.

When I go into Natalie's room the next morning to wake her up for school, I find that she is already out of bed – sitting on the floor, lining up her soft toys in size order. To be honest, she's not that keen on them but people still buy them for her and I don't like the idea of giving them away.

Normally, I would have been pleased that she is playing with them but today I have an important meeting and need to leave on time. Six years with my daughter have taught me what will happen if I try to stop her before she has finished, though.

'Oh Natalie.' I look at my watch in exasperation, and the words are out of my mouth before I can stop them. 'That's *really* helpful.'

Natalie raises her head, a stuffed elephant in her hand and a frown on her face. 'No it isn't.'

I try to keep my voice level. 'I really need you to get dressed, darling. Why don't you finish lining up your toys when you get home from school?'

'I'm not going to school.'

I try to push down the frustration that is welling up in me. I kneel down beside her. 'What do you mean, Natalie? Why not?'

'Because Mrs Pollard is ill and I don't want to go into Mrs Collins' class because she does writing when it should be sums. I told you, Mum.'

'But that was yesterday, Nat. Today will be different.'

I realise as I say it that this is not what my daughter wants to hear. She likes the comfort of things being the same. I'm not sure I can win this argument.

I look out of Natalie's window for inspiration and see, in the distance, Misty's field with the farmhouse behind it.

'I know, Natalie. What if we go and see Misty before school. If we're quick there should be time.'

She thinks for a moment and then nods her head. 'I will like that,' she says, placing the elephant in between a teddy with white fur and an owl with beady eyes.

She goes over to the chair, where I have laid out her school clothes, and starts to get dressed. I breathe a sigh of relief. My boss is accommodating but I have, in the past, had to take days off due to Natalie's school refusal and I worry that at some point he might find it easier to employ someone else.

When Natalie is dressed and has had her breakfast, the same every day – Shreddies with the milk poured up as far as the third blue stripe, we walk the lane to Misty's field.

'He's not there, Mum.'

I step closer to the gate and see that she is right. The field is empty. 'Maybe he's been moved to a different field.'

We walk further along the lane but there is nothing to be seen in the next field except sheep. In the distance, I see the quad bike appear from over the brow of a hill. It accelerates as it makes its way across the field and I feel annoyed that the man we saw yesterday has nothing better to do with his time than buzz around on his toy.

'Come on. We'd better get you to school.'

'You said we could see Misty.'

'I know, darling, but he's not here.'

Natalie plants her feet more firmly. Her voice rises. 'You said!'

'I know I said but I didn't realise Misty wouldn't be here. How about we come back after school?'

A glance at my watch tells me that there is no way I am going to make my meeting. Taking my phone out of my pocket, I punch in my boss's number.

'Frank. Look, sorry but I'm going to have to reschedule this morning's meeting.'

If Frank is annoyed, he hides it well. 'No worries. We'll make it this afternoon. I'm sure Tim won't mind.'

'Thanks, Frank. I appreciate it.'

Natalie sits down on the ground and folds her arms across her chest and I know I'm going to have trouble getting her to move. Frank's voice continues on the end of the phone and it's a moment before I realised that he's still talking. I hear him say my daughter's name.

I look at Natalie, her chin in her cupped hands and her face expressionless. I love my job but more to the point, I need it. 'No, Frank,' I say and I'm surprised at how easily the lie falls from my lips. 'It's nothing to do with Natalie.'

I am just wondering what we are going to do, when a car pulls up alongside us. I'm surprised to see it's Mrs Pollard. Her daughter Clare is in the back; she's a year older than my daughter and Natalie seems to like the older girl.

When Natalie sees them, she stands. 'Hello, Mrs Pollard. You are ill.'

Through the wound down window, Natalie's teacher smiles. 'I *was* ill, Natalie, but I've just been to see the doctor and he says that I am better now and can teach you again. That's why I am running late.'

Natalie walks to the window. 'You're not running. You're in the car.'

'Of course I am, dear. Silly me!'

'Mrs Collins made me do writing instead of sums.'

I raise my eyebrows at Mrs Pollard who simply nods. 'That must have been hard for you, I know.'

'It was,' I say. Without warning, I feel tears stinging my eyes.

'Would you like me to give Natalie a lift to school, Mrs Langley? I always keep a spare booster seat in the back for school trips and I know you have to get off to work. We've got sums first, as always, and then I thought we might do some drawing.'

Natalie's favourite things. I smile gratefully. 'Thank you, Mrs Pollard. That would be very good of you.'

With relief, I watch as Natalie allows herself to be strapped in and blow her a kiss as the car disappears towards the town. Then I turn and walk along the lane. Not the way I came this morning but on towards the farmhouse in the distance.

When the door opens, the dark-haired man I had seen earlier on the quad bike, is standing there. He is dressed in a suit and tie and looks as surprised to see me as I am him.

'It's Mrs Langley,' I start. 'I've come about Misty.'

'Misty?'

I realise that of course he won't know the name Natalie has given the horse in the field. 'The grey horse.'

'Oh,' he says. 'You mean Dunstar.'

'Do you know where he is?'

The man leans against the doorframe. 'Yes,' he says. 'He's gone. He was old...'

I cut him off, a strange anger rising inside me at his words. 'You sold him... because he was old!'

The man takes a step back; his hand makes a stop sign in front of him. 'Woah! I'm not the enemy here. I didn't mean I got rid of him because he was old...' his eyes crease, 'although in a way, I suppose I did.'

I think of the calming effect Misty had on Natalie and the bond there seemed to be between them, stronger than with any human, and feel on the verge of tears.

'My daughter, Natalie, loves that horse.' It's all I can think of to say.

The man puts out a hand then drops it again. 'I know. I've seen her.'

'You mean when you've been swanning around on your rich boy's toy.'

He looks hurt. 'If you mean the quad bike, then I am guilty as charged. I need it to check the sheep. It's quicker than walking and it can go over rougher ground than the truck.'

I feel embarrassed by my outburst. 'I'm sorry, Mr...'

'David,' he says.

'I'm sorry, David. It's just that my daughter has Aspergers and she hates changes. Misty's disappearance is going to hit her hard.'

David looks at me and his hazel eyes are soft. 'It's all right. One of my men has a boy with the syndrome. He talks about him a lot so I know a bit about it.'

'Anyway,' I say. 'If Misty... Dunstar... has gone, then there's nothing to be done.'

I turn away but David calls me back. 'Hey, don't go, Mrs Langley.'

'It's Kathy and there isn't anything more to say. I'll tell her when she gets back from school.'

'But you've only heard half the story. I'm on my way now.'

'On your way?'

'To the place where Misty is. Why don't you come? There's someone I'd like you to meet.'

I look at my watch. 'I'm late for work as it is.'

'Then a few more minutes won't make any difference will they,' he laughs. 'It's not far.'

Later that day, I pick Natalie up from after school club in the car. She stands by the door but won't get in. I can tell she's anxious.

'We don't drive home, Mum. We walk.'

'I know we do, darling, but today we're going somewhere special.'

She looks suspicious. 'I always have a drink when I get home.'

'Then isn't it lucky that I've brought one with me?'

'It wasn't lucky, Mum,' she says, taking it from me. 'You knew you were going to bring it. You took it out of the fridge.'

Reluctantly, Natalie climbs into her booster seat and we drive away from the school. I hope she won't notice that it's not the road we usually take but of course she does. I pre-empt her question.

'We're taking a different road to get to your surprise.'

'I don't like surprises.'

'You'll like this one.'

It's not far and soon we have pulled up outside a collection of buildings. 'Here we are.'

When we get out of the car, Natalie holds back. She doesn't like new places either. 'It's all right, Natalie. There's someone here to see you.'

I lead her to the gate that separates two of the brick buildings. Natalie peers over and then squeals. 'It's Misty!'

'It certainly is,' I say, as David leads the horse across the stable yard. I smile as he approaches. 'Thanks for meeting us here.'

'I wouldn't have missed this for the world,' he says. 'Come on in.'

I push the gate open for Natalie and she runs towards the grey horse. When she reaches him, he ducks his head and rubs his nose against her hand. 'Today we did sums with Mrs Pollard and then we did drawing and then,' she leans closer and cups her hand around the horse's ear, 'I said sorry to Mrs Collins because I screamed at her yesterday.'

David raises his eyebrows and I shrug.

'Would you like to ride him, Natalie?'

She turns to him. 'I would like to ride on him but Mum will say no.'

I laugh. 'Mum will say yes, actually.'

A woman comes out of one of the stables with a riding hat. 'Hello again, Mrs Langley. This ought to fit your daughter.'

We shake hands then she turns to Natalie. 'So this is Natalie. I've heard a lot about you.'

Natalie frowns. 'Why?'

'Because David here says you love horses. Am I right?'

Natalie nods. 'Yes.'

'We are very lucky to have Dunstar, you know.'

'Misty,' David interrupts, looking at Natalie.

'Sorry, yes... Misty. He's a very gentle horse.' She points to a big sign with *Riding For All* written on it in large letters. 'As I said earlier, he's just right for our charity.'

She hands me the riding hat and I put it on Natalie – tightening the strap under her chin.

'I didn't get the chance to tell you before that the people, who come to our stables to ride our horses, have all sorts of different special needs. We are very grateful to David for donating Misty to us... and for agreeing to be one of our patrons.'

David looks a little embarrassed by the praise.

'That's why I was all dressed up when you called round earlier. I'd just had a meeting with the chairman.'

David hadn't mentioned this to me when he'd taken me to the stables earlier to meet Margaret and I'm ashamed of the accusations I made on his doorstep. Feeling myself blush, I look away, hoping David hasn't seen.

Natalie allows Margaret to lift her onto the horse's back and there she sits, my little daughter, as if she owns the world.

David takes the leading reign and walks Misty around the yard. He certainly looks more comfortable in his check shirt and jeans than he did in a suit and tie.

As she passes me, Natalie gives a wave.

'Look at me, Mum!' She leans her head towards Misty's ear and turns her face to me.

'That's my mum,' she says, patting his grey neck. For a fleeting moment our eyes lock, '... and I love her.'

NEW BEGINNINGS

New beginnings, Angie thought as she looked out of her daughter's kitchen window at the buds just forming on the ornamental cherry. She smiled and hugged her arms around herself remembering Alex's tiny fingers curled around her own and his soft downy head.

Friends had told her that a first grandchild was special, but until this tiny little baby had been placed in her arms, she had not fully understood.

'What do you think, Mum?' Jessie had asked, her hair damp on the pillow but her eyes shining. 'Isn't he just perfect?'

'Yes, he is,' Angie had agreed. 'He really is.'

Angie had held the little bundle close to her chest and rocked him gently.

'I'm your nan, Alex, and I'll always be there for you, just like I was for your mum. You must always remember that.'

Out of the corner of her eye, she had seen Jessie shaking her head and chuckling to Den but she didn't care. She had meant every word.

The beep of her mobile made her jump. She found her reading glasses and looked at the screen.

1 message received.

Angie stared at the words for a moment, confused. The message said it was from Alex. She pressed the read button and the message appeared.

Dear Nan. Thanks for helping Mummy when I was being born. She was too tired to tell you herself but I know she was glad you were there. Everything is so strange and big but I know I am going to love this world. Love Alex

Angie smiled to herself. Only a day after giving birth and there was Jessie thinking of others and helping to light up their day, as usual.

Den and Jessie had been waiting a long time for a baby and, now that he was here, their lives were complete. She remembered her daughter's heartache at the two losses she had had the previous year, first her beloved father and then a miscarriage at ten weeks but Angie had shared her joy when six months later Jessie had found out she was expecting again.

She and Den had asked her to go with them to the ultrasound screening and Angie had driven down from her home in Norfolk to the hospital. Once there, she had shed tears of relief and happiness at the sight of the small outline of her grandson on the screen.

When they had found out, in the eighth month, that Alex wasn't thriving and was going to have to be induced early, she had been sick with worry but Jessie had been upbeat. *He'll be fine, Mum. You worry too much.*

Typical Jessie. Always so positive, her glass always half full. Angie wondered where her daughter got her strength – it certainly wasn't from her. But of course, Jessie's father had been optimistic too – a fixer of problems right until the end. Her daughter had been right all along: Alex had entered the world tiny but with the spirit of his grandfather. She was sad Ralph was no longer with them to meet his tiny grandson.

But today was not a day for sadness, she thought, remembering how full her heart had been as she kissed the soft fuzz on the top of Alex's head – it was a time for celebration: the present was rosy and Ralph would have been so proud.

The following day, Angie awoke to the beep of her phone telling her she had a message. She fumbled on the bedside table for her glasses.

Dear Nan. I was a very good boy and only woke Mum up three times last night! Mum is a bit tired now but I am wide-awake and think that it might be time for some more milk. The nurses are very kind. I like the one with the smiley face best. Love Alex

Although it was only five thirty, Angie chuckled. She remembered how Jessie had wanted feeding every three hours and had grown out of her newborn sleep suits within days. It looked as though Alex would take after his mother in that respect. She would go over to the hospital and see them that afternoon. Already she could feel a need stir within her – the need to stroke Alex's soft cheek.

When Angie arrived at Jessie's ward, Den had gone to the cafeteria to get a drink and Jessie was asleep. Alex lay in his cot beside the bed and Angie could just see his tiny fist waving above the plastic side.

'Hello, little man,' she said lifting him gently out of the cot. 'It's your Nan.'

Alex opened his mouth and closed it again, screwing up his face.

'Just like your grandad,' she whispered to him.

Jessie stirred and rubbed her eyes with her hand.

'Hi Mum. How long have you been here?'

'Only about ten minutes. I was taking the chance to get to know this little fellow while his mother was asleep.'

Jessie winced as she sat up and Angie looked worriedly at her daughter. She settled herself on the chair next to the bed, Alex cradled against her shoulder.

'Are you okay?'

'Of course I'm okay, just a little sore and tired. What do you expect, Mum.' Jessie mustered up a smile and patted Angie on her arm. 'I've just had a baby.'

Angie smoothed Jessie's fringe from her eyes. 'I know you have and you're going to be a brilliant mother, Jess. I just wish I could stay down here a bit longer and be there for you when you come out tomorrow but I can't really take any more time off.'

Angie had been at Jessie and Den's for over a week now, arriving just before her daughter's due date and helping to keep her entertained through the long days of waiting until Alex had decided to make his appearance ten days later. She was due to go back home the next day and it felt like a wrench.

'I wish I could stay longer,' she said, lowering Alex back into his cot, 'but it will give you space to be a family – just you, Den and Alex.'

The following week, Angie was leaving the house to go to her book club when her phone beeped. She had got used to Alex's messages and looked forward to their updates: so cheery and positive and so like Jessie.

She had been back a week and Angie had phoned Jessie as much as she dared; she didn't want her daughter to think she was interfering. The phone calls followed a similar pattern – she would ask if Jessie was getting enough sleep or whether her stitches were bothering her or how long Alex was going between feeds. Jessie's answers were always the same.

'We're fine, Mum and, yes, Alex is fine too – you worry too much.'

Angie took her phone out of her bag. She'd read the text quickly before she left.

Dear Nan. I am finding it hard to sleep even though Mum sings to me and rocks me. I don't mean to make her tired but I miss her when she puts me down in my cot. Maybe I'll sleep better tomorrow. Love Alex

Angie stood with the phone in her hands wondering what to make of the text. It made her uneasy and she dialled Jessie's number.

The phone rang for a while and when Jessie eventually answered she sounded distracted.

'Oh, hi Mum.'

'How is everything, Jessie?'

'Everything's fine, I was just trying to have a nap. Den's taken Alex out in the pram to give me a break.'

'You would tell me if anything was wrong, wouldn't you?'

'Of course I would.' Her daughter's voice sounded distant. 'You worry too much, Mum.'

'Well, I'll let you get some rest but let me know if you want me to come back down. I'm sure I can get Keith to juggle the roster.'

'Don't be silly. Everything's great. I'll talk to you tomorrow.'

Angie stood looking at the phone. She should have felt reassured, Jessie had said everything was fine, but Alex's text had unsettled her.

At the book group, Angie proudly handed round the photos of Alex she had taken a few hours after he was born. His dark blue eyes stared out from his perfect face and his features were delicate, like Jessie's.

'You must be so proud,' her friend Sarah said, handing back the photo. 'How's Jessie doing? It's a big change for her, being at home looking after a baby after all those years of working full time.'

'She's doing great – coping well. Just like she always does,' Angie replied, but she was aware that her answer lacked conviction.

That night, Angie found it hard to get to sleep and when she did, she dreamt that Jessie was in the sea, her arms reaching out to her through the waves. The night passed slowly and when she woke the next morning, her bed clothes were tangled around her legs and one of her pillows was on the floor. She was relieved that it was the weekend. She looked at her phone – no messages.

Feeling strangely restless, Angie decided to visit the Saturday market but every few minutes she found herself checking her phone. She was used to an update from Alex each morning and sometimes again in the evening but today the screen remained blank. Should she ring Jessie? No, she was being silly – a worrier – as Jessie would say.

In the afternoon, Angie decided to do some gardening. The rain they'd had the previous night had softened the earth and she planned to weed around the fresh green shoots of the hyacinths that had started to push through under the apple tree. She was just putting on her gardening gloves, when her phone beeped in her pocket. It must be Alex's message. She breathed a sigh of relief but when she looked at the screen, she saw that the message was from Sarah.

As she pulled out the straggly weeds from around the bulbs, the soil felt claggy and heavy under her fingers and she took no satisfaction in the task. A strange gnawing disquiet had started to form in the pit of her stomach.

It was eleven o'clock and Angie sat in bed, her mobile in her hand. She put it down again: it wouldn't do to disturb Jessie this late. *I'll ring in the morning and Jessie will tell me I've been silly*, she thought to herself. Turning the light off, she closed her eyes but sleep wouldn't come. As she lay awake, she wondered again why Alex hadn't sent his usual messages. An idea started to form. Reaching across to her bedside table, she picked up her mobile and, pressing the text button, started to write.

Dear Alex. It is very late and I hope you are asleep, and Mummy too. But if you are awake, I want to tell you something important. If you need me, for anything at all, or if you are worried about Mummy, you must tell me straight away. You will do that for me, won't you, Alex? From your loving Nan x

Then she turned off the bedside light, closed her eyes and drifted into a fitful sleep.

It was just after three when her phone beeped its message. Angie shot up in bed. She grabbed the mobile and looked at the screen.

1 message received.

Greedily, she clicked the read button.

Dear Nan. Please come and see me. I think I need you to be here for a while. Love Alex

Angie leapt out of bed and pulled on her clothes. It was still dark outside and a watery moon hung low in the sky. To her relief, the car started immediately. It would be a long drive but the thought didn't worry her.

Den opened the door. Alex was in his arms, his head on his father's shoulder. His tiny face was red but his eyes were closed.

'He's just gone,' Den said, opening the door wider for Angie to come in. 'Jessie's just fed him but he

30

only goes two hours between feeds. She's shattered – we both are.' He sank down onto the settee. 'It's since I've been back at work – Jess is finding it hard to adjust to being at home alone with the baby.'

'Here let me take him,' Angie said. 'I'll put him back in his cot then go and see Jessie.'

As Angie walked into her daughter's bedroom, she could see Jessie half propped up on the pillows, her eyes red and swollen. She sat down on the bed.

'Why didn't you tell me you weren't coping?' she said gently.

'I didn't want you to worry,' Jessie said, with a sniff. 'Everyone expects me to be so strong.'

'There's no weakness in asking for help. Sometimes it's good to have someone else to sort out the problems. I told Alex I would be there for him and I meant it.' She smiled at her daughter.

'I know, Mum and I'm glad. But how come you're here in the middle of the night? Did Den ask you to come?'

Angie raised her eyebrows. 'But I thought it was you…'

'No. I gave Den my phone so that I wouldn't be tempted to call you.'

Angie frowned. There was a sound in the doorway and Den stood there looking sheepish, Jessie's phone in his hand.

She looked at her son-in-law, understanding at last. 'No, Den didn't ask me to come,' she smiled. 'Alex did.'

THE TOAST OF MAIDA VALE

When the piece of toast with the face of Jesus popped out of the toaster, it looked just like any other piece of toast – or so Margaret thought as she took it out and placed it on her plate ready for buttering.

It wasn't that she was expecting this piece of bread to be any different to the thousands she had toasted before in her spotless kitchen with its artfully distressed wooden cabinets with their granite worktops – or even wishing for it. But as it lay there waiting to be smeared with monounsaturated spread, on the fashionably square breakfast plate that she had bought from Next, there was no mistaking the resemblance.

She stood back and viewed the toast from a different angle – maybe she had been mistaken. But no, as she studied the hues and shades of the toasted surface there could be no mistaking the strong nose, the flowing hair and the dark shadow of beard along the jaw. It was Jesus as clear as day.

Margaret was disappointed when Brian didn't show as much enthusiasm as she did. 'Can't you see, Brian? There are his cheek bones and there's no mistaking his eyes.'

'They're sunflower seeds, Maggie. I told you to buy the white sliced.'

But Margaret was having none of it. The toast was a sign – left for her, in her kitchen in Maida Vale.

'A sign of what?' Brian asked but Margaret knew that he wouldn't understand.

'That things are about to change.'

Brian reached for the plate but she batted his hand away. 'You mustn't touch it!'

'But I'm hungry.'

'Then you'll have to have cornflakes. You can't eat it... it's special.'

'It's a piece of toasted rye and sunflower bread, Maggie – that's all. Look, this wouldn't be something to do with Adam would it?'

Adam was their son. The week before, he had slipped out of the house, under the cover of darkness with her Avon money and a packet of Waitrose pecan and maple biscuits, and they hadn't seen him since. Not a word. Not even a postcard.

At first she had missed him – like she might have missed a limb – but after a few days she rather liked the tidy hallway where his size eleven shoes had been thrown and the way she no longer listened out for his constant requests for tea or pot noodles. It was also rather nice not to have to lie awake at night and listen to him fall through the door after a night at the pub

No, this new event had nothing to do with Adam. She picked up the Jesus toast by its corner, between thumb and finger.

'I think we should have this looked at. It could be as important as the Turin Shroud.'

She went to the drawer and took out a roll of Clingfilm. Tearing some off, she carefully wrapped the toast in it then propped it up on the worktop.

'Looked at by who, might I ask?' Brian said, heaving his rather large backside off the breakfast barstool.

'I don't know. The vicar or someone.'

'But you don't know the vicar – you don't even go to church.'

'Well, I'll look it up on the internet... there must be some expert in this field. What would he be called?'

'A psychiatrist, I should think,' Brian muttered.

For four days the toast stood on the worktop next to the kettle and every day, the likeness grew stronger to Margaret. She found that she would sometimes have a little chat to the face as she went to boil the kettle or take a carton of milk from the fridge.

On day five, Lillian, Margaret's neighbour, called round. 'I've popped over to see if you've heard anything. You know, about Adam.'

'Adam is a good boy,' she replied. 'He'll come home when he's ready.'

Lillian said nothing and Margaret knew she was remembering the time when her son had sprayed water from the hose over the fence while she had been sunbathing. His explanation that she had looked hot had not gone down too well.

'I suppose he is an adult. Must have decided it was time to fly the nest and make his own way in the world.'

Adam was in fact thirty-two but Margaret didn't think it was the time to remind Lillian of that... or to mention the Avon money.

'I want to show you something, Lillian.'

Margaret took her neighbour's arm and led her to where the toast was propped up against the biscuit tin.

'Why are you showing me your breakfast, Maggie?'

'It's not my breakfast, it's a miracle... look.'

Margaret held the toast, in its cling film, up for her to see. 'Don't tell me you can't see it!'

'Give me a clue,' Lillian said, leaning her elbows on the counter.

'It's Jesus. Look at the way his robes are folded – it's exquisite.'

Lillian took the toast from her. 'Yes, there certainly is some likeness,' she said, holding it up to the light.

'I've phoned the local paper. They're coming to interview me this afternoon. They say that we're pretty low on miracles in Maida Vale – especially at this time of the year. I can hardly believe it.'

It wasn't a bad photograph when it appeared in the *Wood and Vale*. Margaret had put on her best blouse, the one that she had bought in the Harrods sale, and had tried to wear her most pious expression. *The Weeping Toast of Maida Vale!* shouted the headline.

Margaret didn't recall having told them that the face in the toast had actually wept but if she looked closely there was a line of seeds that could have been mistaken for the trace of a tear.

It was after the local radio station interviewed her that she was first stopped in the street. The woman wheeled her shopping trolley into her path and looked at her with expectant eyes.

'Tell me. How did you feel when you saw Jesus looking up at you from your breakfast plate?'

Margaret told the woman that she had felt very honoured, thank you very much, to be chosen as the recipient of such a miracle. When pushed, she had also told her the make and price of the loaf and the store where she had bought it.

It wasn't long before she and Brian started to notice people hanging about on the pavement in front of their house.

'What are they doing?' her husband asked and she had smiled at him indulgently.

'They are here to see me, Brian,' was all she had said.

Margaret took to finding excuses to go out onto the doorstep: the milk needed bringing in or the windows needed cleaning. She started checking her appearance in the mirror before she opened the door and if anyone was waiting there, would raise her hand in a gesture of benevolent greeting.

One morning, as she stepped outside to bring in the cat, a young boy was pushed forwards by his mother.

'Go on. That's the toast lady. Get her to sign your book.'

It had pleased Margaret more than she could say to write her name next to that of someone called John, who she was told had played a cyber man in an episode of Doctor Who.

Another time, someone crossed the street and handed her a bag of sliced white. 'Could you toast me a Jesus too, do you think?'

Brian wasn't happy, though, especially when tents started to appear on the land designated as Green Space at the end of their road. 'Don't you think this has gone a bit far, Maggie? It's not as if it's going to bring him home.'

'I told you. It's nothing to do with Adam,' Margaret said. She was thinking about whether a spritz of hairspray might preserve the face – in the last day or so, she had noticed it looking rather tired and there was a slight green tinge to the edges if you looked closely enough.

'I think we should tell the police,' Brian flinched at the icy look Margaret threw him but carried on, 'about the missing money.'

Margaret didn't want to think about the money, though – or Adam. She had spent the best years of her life caring for him and bailing him out when times got hard. It was her time now. The toast had turned her into a minor celebrity in the district and she was enjoying every second of it.

When Adam let himself into the house, the following night, after ten days on his mate's lumpy couch, he couldn't help but feel a little relieved to be back. He'd missed his mother's cooking and the way she let him sleep in on a weekend. She even did all his washing. He was sure he could explain away the Avon money – make up a pregnant girlfriend or something.

He had been rather disconcerted to find that he had to step over a sleeping reporter on the doorstep and as he had put his key in the lock, a woman had called out from across the road to him, 'Are you the son of Toast Lady?'

The lights were out in the kitchen and all was quiet. Boy was he hungry – Kevin's attempts at cooking were best forgotten and there were only so many Big Macs a grown man could eat.

Adam was rather surprised that the toast, when he came upon it on the worktop, was wrapped in Clingfilm and it had the rather unusual smell of lacquer. But beggars couldn't be choosers and smeared with a lavish dollop of maple syrup it went down a treat.

As he wiped the crumbs from his mouth with his sleeve, he thought of his mother asleep upstairs. How she must have missed him – but he was home now and things could get back to just the way they were before he had left.

He couldn't wait to see the look on her face the next morning.

JUST MAYBE

For a moment Kate allowed herself to believe that the holiday might bring their two families together.

Below the terraced garden of the villa, the olive trees were bent like old men. She rested her arms on the stonewall and breathed in the sweet scent of the jasmine that, despite being September, was still in full bloom. Behind her, a yellow lilo drifted across the pool. Bliss.

'If I find you've taken my iPod, you'll wish you'd never been born!'

Kate sighed. She knew she had been optimistic in expecting the peace to last. Turning back towards the open patio doors that led out onto the pool terrace, she could just make out Lilly, her stepdaughter, striding through the living area, her hair wrapped up in an orange towel.

'I haven't got it!' Ben's voice was plaintive. 'It wasn't me.'

'I'm going to search your room and if I find you've had it, I'll break your transformer into a million pieces.'

Kate could hear Ben start to cry and it wasn't long before his little form appeared in the doorway. 'Mum, Lilly said that...'

'I know, Ben. I heard.'

Kate sighed again. Whoever thought that a late summer holiday to Greece for the children to 'bond' was a good idea, must have needed their head examining. She could still hear Neil's voice in her head. *They just don't get to spend enough time together, that's all. They'll all be the best of friends by the end of the week, you just see.*

But it had been like this from the moment they had touched down at Kerkyra airport.

'I thought you'd organised a hire car?' Kate had looked accusingly at her husband.

'No. You said you were. That and the boat hire.'

'I didn't book that either.'

Lilly had raised her eyebrows and stared pointedly at Kate. 'Typical. *My* mum wouldn't have forgotten.'

'Why don't you take a long hike, Lilly!' Tam's voice took Kate by surprise. She knew it was wrong but as she watched her son glare at his stepsister, she couldn't help but feel pleased with the way he had taken her side.

In the end they had waited over an hour, in the mid-day heat, until a taxi, large enough to accommodate the whole family, had became available. If it hadn't been for Ben's travel sickness and the fact that the baby hadn't stopped crying since they'd arrived, the scenic drive to the village where they were staying would have been pleasurable.

Kate idly pushed the yellow lilo out across water with her toe, then skirted the pool and made her way back inside.

'Try to be nice to Lilly,' she said, ushering Ben back inside, 'and she'll be nice to you.'

'But she's never nice. She said that even ants have bigger brains than me.'

'Well, that's just her way. She doesn't mean it.'

'I *do*.' Lilly's voice could just be heard over the whine of the hairdryer.

Tam, was lying across the settee, in just a pair of knee length swimming shorts, his hair obscuring his face and one flip-flop dangling from his size ten foot. Beside him, lay what looked like Lilly's iPod. Kate threw him a warning look but he ignored it.

'Where's your dad?' she asked.

Tam looked up from the magazine he was reading. There was a pause before he spoke. 'He's not my dad.'

The basket under the buggy was bulging with towels, sun cream, nappies, sting relief, the baby's bottles and all manner of other things needed when you were silly enough to embark on a holiday abroad with young children. The older two had their own rucksacks slung over their shoulders.

The wheels of the buggy were forming ever-deeper trenches in the pebbles as Kate struggled to push it.

'Here, let me.'

She was relieved when Neil took hold of the frame, picking it up, baby and all, and carrying it to an empty spot beside a small jetty – its weathered legs mirrored in the water.

'Will this do?' He parked the buggy and pulled out a blanket from the basket underneath, which he spread out across the stones.

Tam took off his T-shirt and threw himself onto his stomach. 'Why couldn't we have gone to a beach with sun beds and umbrellas like most people? I suppose it was *his* idea,' he said, looking at Neil, before plugging the earphones of Lilly's iPod into his ears. Kate shot him a look and took Neil's hand.

Neil shook his head. 'Don't worry about it.'

He lifted the baby out of his buggy and placed him on the rug. Neil was so forgiving – that was what she loved most about him. She knew she should say something to her son about his behaviour but what with Ben and the baby she didn't have the energy.

'Hey, that's mine!' Lilly, her face red with anger and from the previous day's sun, snatched the white cables from out of Tam's ears and with a glare that could fell an army, stormed off along the beach. She threw her towel down on the pebbles as far away from them as possible.

'And don't even think about following me,' she shouted back at Ben who had started to trail behind her on his short legs.

'So much for happy families,' Kate thought.

The beach was virtually empty, other families preferring the sun beds and tavernas of the neighbouring larger bays.

'Who's for a swim? Tam?' Tam ignored him. He was still sprawled on his front on the rug and Ben was decorating his back with stones. 'What about you, Kate?'

Kate stopped bouncing baby Zak on her knees. She was struggling to keep him from snatching off his sun hat. She felt hot and irritable. 'How can I, Neil? Use your common sense.'

From his position on the rug, Tam gave a snigger and Kate felt guilty as she watched a shadow pass fleetingly across her husband's face. Neil does mind, she thought to herself. He just tries not to show it; all he wants is for us to be a proper family.

'Not to worry,' her husband said, mustering a smile. 'I'll let you know what the water's like.'

Lilly lay on her back, an arm flung over her eyes. The sun beat down on her skin but she couldn't muster the energy to put on more sun cream. She was so bored. When her dad had told her they were going to Corfu for their holiday, if truth be told, she had been quite excited, despite the fact that it would mean spending a week with her stepmother and her children. Her imagination had dreamed up sun soaked, sandy beaches; the sound of bouzouki music from local bars and a surfeit of gorgeous Greek waiters to flatter her.

The reality couldn't have been further from this picture. Their villa was marooned on the side of some god-forsaken hill with nothing but olive trees for neighbours and instead of sand, the beach was made of pebbles that dug into her back when she tried to sunbathe. The nearest thing they had to a taverna was *Dimitri*'s, which was little more than a shack on the corner where the track from their villa met the small seafront road. Dimitri himself must have been almost sixty and not quite what she'd had in mind.

Squinting back down the beach, she watched Kate bounce Zak on her knees. She supposed that the baby was quite cute, even though she didn't like to admit it. It wasn't his fault that his mother was someone she wished had never entered her life and that his birth had put the final nail in the coffin of her mum and dad ever getting back together.

'Kalimera.'

Lilly jumped. Apart from her family, she hadn't known that anyone else was on the tiny beach. She turned her head towards the voice but the sun was dazzling and she could only make out the silhouette of the speaker's body against the washed out sky.

'You are English?' The owner of the voice squatted down next to her and she was aware of brown legs clad in cut-off denims. As she put on her sunglasses, the boy's face swam into view and Lilly was glad she had, as they stopped him from seeing the surprise in her eyes. She'd never seen such a beautiful smile and the way his brown eyes crinkled when he did so, made her stomach turn over.

'You are the new family at Villa Anna?' he asked.

'Yes, we got here two days ago.'

'You like?' His brown arm swooped an arc to encompass the sea and the small cove, the hills behind peppered with olive trees.

'It's um... well it's...'

'I know,' he said, his brown eyes twinkling. 'You think it is not fun here. I used to think that, when I lived here but now that I have moved away to the mainland for my studies, I miss it very much.'

Lilly propped herself up on one elbow. 'So your family live here?'

He hesitated. 'Only my uncle now – he owns the taverna on the corner. I stay with him in the summer and help him out. I'm Stephan by the way.'

'Your uncle is Dimitri?' Things were beginning to look up.

He nodded. 'And this is your family?' He gestured to the small group at the other end of the beach.

Lilly frowned. 'They like to think so – that's my dad in the sea. I suppose the baby's partly my family too.'

Stephan looked puzzled. 'And the lady?'

'Oh,' she said, lying back down on the towel. 'That's just the woman Dad married.'

Kate tucked Ben into his bed and kissed him goodnight. 'Dad and I are just popping out to the supermarket in the next town, Ben. We won't be long and Lilly will look after you.'

'I don't want Lilly,' Ben said, sitting up. 'I want Tam.'

'Tam's not back yet.'

Tam had taken himself off along the path that led through the olive groves to the next bay where a handful of tavernas clung to the water's edge. Kate had wanted him to stay and share their family meal, but he had just tied his jumper around his waist and let himself out the back door. Her call for him to be back before it got dark, as he didn't have a torch, went unheeded.

'Why couldn't I have gone too?' Lilly had asked as they were eating dinner on the terrace later.

'Because,' Neil replied, 'Tam is eighteen and you're not.'

'I can't believe you, Dad.' Lilly threw down her fork and ran into the bedroom, the sound of the slamming door echoing around the hills.

Now Kate needed to find a way to reassure Ben. They could take the baby with them, but the little boy had nearly fallen asleep over his *baklava* after a day of sea and sun and there was no way they could take him. 'You'll be fine with Lilly, Ben. You're nearly seven now and anyway, we'll be back before you know it. You want sausages for the barbeque tomorrow don't you?'

It was a cheap trick, as Kate knew that sausages were Ben's favourite food in the world, but it worked and he reluctantly allowed her to kiss him goodnight and close the curtains.

'Can you mind Ben for a bit, Lilly?' Her father's head peered round her bedroom door. 'Mum and I are just...'

Lilly looked daggers at him. 'Don't call her that!'

'I'm sorry.' She was pleased to see that her father looked embarrassed. 'Kate and I are going to the supermarket for tomorrow's barbeque. We'll be about an hour and a half.'

'But I said I'd...' Lilly stopped. She wasn't sure how her father would react to the news that she had planned to meet Stephan at *Dimitri's*. Her heart skipped a beat as she remembered the way he'd looked at her before he had left to help his uncle with the lunches. *We will sit on my uncle's terrace and I will show you the way the stars pierce the sky like a million tiny pin pricks.* This was a far cry from the crass language used by the boys she hung around with at school.

It would be best if he didn't know about her arrangement – after all, Tam would be back soon and then he could take over the babysitting. She looked at her watch. Thirty minutes until she had said she'd meet him. Plenty of time.

'Okay, but tell him he's not allowed out of bed. I'm sick of him following me around – it was bad enough having to sit next to him on the plane.'

'Oh. Lilly,' her father sighed. 'Can't you make an effort... just this once?'

Lilly's answer was to turn her back on her father and carry on filing her nails until with a backwards glance at his daughter, he left the room and closed the door. Lilly put down the nail file and bit at the skin around her nails, a habit she thought she had grown out of. She was still angry. How could Dad have let Tam go to the next village while she had to stay behind and babysit? She was his daughter after all, his child... his *real* child.

Lilly stood by the window and willed Tam to walk through the side gate and onto the pool terrace. It was gone eight and the sun was already sinking behind the silvery green hills. Stephan would be wondering where she was. She had told him that her Dad and Kate were okay with her walking down to the taverna, even though she knew that if she had told them, they would never have let her go. She hadn't wanted to look like a baby. Her plan had been to plead a headache and stay in her room, secure in the knowledge that her stepmother was unlikely to check on her.

She glanced at Ben's door. If it wasn't for him, she'd be sitting on the terrace at *Dimitri's*, drinking ouzo and looking at the stars with the best-looking guy in Corfu. The usual mix or resentment and jealousy rose in her stomach. Tiptoeing to the door, she opened it a crack. Ben was fast asleep, one hand clutching the worn blanket he refused to give up. She looked at her watch again. If she popped down to the taverna for just half an hour, who'd know? She'd be back before her dad and Kate and anyway Tam would be back soon.

Closing Ben's door quietly and grabbing her bag from the back of the chair, she quietly left the villa and made her way down the track to *Dimitri's*. If she had turned her head she might have seen the small face of Ben at his bedroom window.

Lilly leant back in the old wicker chair and with her fingers tapped out a rhythm on its arms to the Greek music that was playing through the speakers on *Dimitri's* terrace. The ouzo was making her light headed.

'It's great to be away from them all... the family I mean.'

When Stephan didn't reply, she at first thought that he hadn't heard. 'I said...'

'You are lucky to have a big family.' His answer was blunt. Lilly opened her eyes and looked across at him. He was looking away into the distance where, through the olive trees, glimpses of the sea, dark green in the fading light could just be seen.

'I wouldn't exactly say I was lucky.' She was aware that her voice sounded childish.

'Believe me,' he said, steepling his fingers under his chin, 'you are.'

The mood had changed from the light-hearted conversation they'd had when she'd first arrived. Lilly wondered if it was something she'd said. His expression was sad. Maybe there was a way to make him smile his gorgeous smile again.

'You wouldn't believe some of the annoying things my step brother Ben has done.'

She was surprised when Stephan excused himself and went back inside the taverna. Wondering whether it was the right thing to do, Lilly followed him. A delicious smell of lamb and tomatoes met her as she walked into the small dining area. A few of the tables were occupied and around the walls were photographs; Stephan was nowhere to be seen.

One of the photographs was larger than the rest. In it was a good-looking man, his smile familiar to her, and a woman with long black hair. Lilly presumed these were Stephan's parents. In front of them stood two boys. The taller of the two had his hand resting protectively on the shoulder of the younger boy.

'My sister and her family.' Lilly had not heard Dimitri coming up behind her. He started to light the candles on the tables.

'Is that Stephan?' she asked, indicating the older boy.

'Yes, and that is his younger brother, Andre.'

'Are they very close?'

Dimitri turned away and continued to light the candles. 'They were,' he said, 'until the accident. Stephan hasn't told you?'

Lilly shook her head. 'No, he hasn't told me anything about his family.'

'It is a very sad story. Maybe Stephan would not want me to...'

'It's all right Uncle.' Stephan took Lilly by the hand. 'I will tell her the story.'

He led Lilly back onto the terrace, which was dark now apart from the coloured lights that were wound through the canopy of vines above their heads. 'I went to get this.' He handed Lilly a photograph of a young boy, his smile, just like Stephan's, lighting up the picture.

'He was six,' he said lowering his head. 'I was ten and I was supposed to have been looking after him. He loved the water – he could swim like a fish and would have stayed in the sea all day if our mother had let him. On the day he died, there was a strong current. A few of us were helping my uncle out by mending his nets. I never saw him go in the water... and I never saw him again.'

'But you were only ten... you couldn't have known.'

Stephan ran a hand down his face. 'I miss him every day. Like I said... you are lucky with your family. You are blessed.'

Lilly thought of Ben in his bed, his small hand clutching his blanket. Something inside her stirred. He was only six and he'd had to cope with losing someone in his life when his father left. Was this why he had craved affection from her – his stepsister? She gasped. She had left Ben alone in the villa... and that villa had a pool.

'I've got to go, Stephan!' Lilly snatched up her bag and ran from the taverna.

She took off her heels and raced barefoot towards the lights of the villa. When she threw herself breathless into the living room, the house was quiet. Tam was not back yet and neither were her dad and Kate. Relief flooded through her. Quietly, she opened the door to Ben's room... he was not there.

'Ben! Ben! Where are you?'

Lilly raced from room to room. Moonlight fell in rectangles through the panes of glass in the patio doors and beyond, Lilly could see its reflection in the surface of the pool. *Please God*, she thought, *don't let it be true*. Her hand was shaking as she flung open the doors. The water lay still and motionless and it was impossible for Lilly to see what secrets it held beneath its flat surface.

'Lilly.'

Lilly spun round. Ben stood in the doorway, his blanket clutched to his face.

'Ben!' Lilly grabbed the boy to her. 'Where were you? Are you all right?'

Ben gave a yawn. 'I went into Mum's room to see where she was and fell asleep on her bed. Will you read me a story, Lilly?'

Kate glanced at her watch as she put down Zak's car seat and fumbled in her bag for the keys to the villa. 'Lilly will be wondering where we've got to.'

'Well, we would have been back sooner if it hadn't been for Tam.' Neil supported Tam under his arm. 'Your mum told you to take a torch – good job you were sensible enough to head for the main road or who knows what might have happened. Lucky we were passing.'

Kate found the keys and let them into the villa. All was quiet. Lilly wasn't anywhere to be seen so she presumed she'd taken herself off to bed. When she heard voices coming from Ben's room, she was surprised. She opened the door. Ben was sitting up in bed, his thumb in his mouth and his other hand enclosed in Lilly's.

'And so you see, Ben, the big, green giant didn't need to be frightened any more.'

Kate closed the door as quietly as she could. Her eldest son was sprawled in his usual position on the settee and Neil was bandaging his foot. 'I think that next time you want to go to the next village, I'll give you a lift.'

'Thanks, Neil,' Tam said, clapping his stepfather on the back. 'That's cool. Maybe I'll let Lilly come with me.'

Kate picked Zak out of his car seat and held him close. There was a nugget of hope inside her. *Maybe* she thought. *Just maybe.*

LINKS IN A CHAIN

Erin's mother, Janet, lifted the fine gold chain and fastened it around her daughter's neck, 'I think it's perfect,' she said. 'Happy birthday, darling.'

Erin looked at herself in the rectangular hand-mirror that the jeweller was holding up and marvelled at the tiny links and the way the necklace sat perfectly at the base of her collarbones.

'Do you like it?' her mother asked, a tiny crease between her brows and Erin knew how important it was for her that she did. Her father had died when she was only young and their shared grief, and gradual rebuilding of their lives, had brought them all the closer.

She turned her head a fraction and held her mother's eyes, dark like her own, in the mirror. 'Of course I like it, Mum – it's just like yours.'

Ever since she could remember, Erin had loved her mother's gold chain. As a child, she had sat on her lap, as Postman Pat did his rounds on the television, one finger in her mouth and the other tracing the fine gold links around her mother's throat. She knew that her grandmother had given it to her on her eighteenth birthday and as far as she knew, her mother had never taken it off.

'Not even in the bath?' she'd asked, incredulous.

'No, not even there,' her mother had laughed. 'One day, when you're grown up, I'll buy you your own gold necklace and when you no longer live here, you can feel the chain around your neck, and know that you are never far away from me in my thoughts.' She ran the fine chain between her finger and thumb. 'It will link us always.'

'But it won't need to. I'm never leaving home, Mum. I'm going to live here forever.'

Her mother had laughed. 'One day I think you'll change your mind,' was all she had said.

Erin had longed for the day when she would be eighteen and could stand with her mother in the jewellers shop and now that day had come.

'No, I'll keep it on thanks,' she said to the jeweller, putting the empty little box he had given her, into her bag. 'I don't intend to ever take it off.'

Her mother smiled. 'Be careful with it though, Erin. The links are so fine that they'll easily break.'

For as long as Erin could remember, she had been accident-prone. Things seemed to break whenever she was near them and, over the years, her mother had been exasperated at the number of times the arms of her glasses had got bent or the buttons had pinged off her coat.

'Don't worry, Mum. I'll be just as careful as you've been with yours.'

And she had been careful – just as she had promised. She never took the necklace off, not for swimming or even when she went to bed. Even when she had bought one of the chunky beaded necklaces which had become so popular, it had just lain on top of the chain, the gold glinting from between the plastic baubles.

Erin had travelled around Europe in her gap year and if, from time to time, she had felt a little unsure of herself or had fallen out with her travelling companions, it had only taken a touch of the necklace for her to feel that connection with home.

A year later, she had packed her things and her mother had driven her to her university campus. Standing in the corridor of the halls of residence, watching her mother walk away, an empty feeling had started to grow inside her, and without thinking, she had rubbed the thin chain between her thumb and finger. As her mother's figure had grown smaller, she could see by the angle of her arm that she was doing the same thing.

But now, the unthinkable had happened. Erin had woken up to find the necklace no longer around her neck. She dived under the flowered duvet in her little room, with its desk and the row of cacti along the windowsill, and searched for it. When she found it wasn't there, she lay on the worn blue carpet, between her piles of lecture notes and textbooks, and stared into the gloom under her bed. It was hopeless. The necklace was so fine that it would be impossible to see in the chaos of her room and when she thought about it, she wasn't even sure when she had last been aware of it around her neck – it might have been days since she'd lost it.

Erin groaned and felt the empty space beneath her collarbones and as she stood there in the clutter, it was as if the invisible thread that bound her to her mother had been broken and that she was floating adrift in a way she had never felt before. But what was worse was the knowledge that when she went home to visit that weekend, she would have to watch her mother's face fall as she told her.

Janet sprinkled the food on top of the water and watched the fish swim up to nibble it, their mouths gaping and their bodies distorted in the glass. She jumped as the telephone rang with a sharp trill and she replaced the lid of the tank. As she went to answer it, her hand moved subconsciously to her throat and the thin gold chain that lay there.

'Hello, dear,' her mother said. 'I won't keep you, but I just wondered whether you had lost your gold chain. I found one here this morning; it was down the side of the chair. I don't know how long it's been there but it looks a lot like yours. The catch is broken.'

Even though Janet knew that her own chain was safely around her neck, her hand still shot to her throat.

'No, it's not mine, Mum.'

'Could it be Erin's do you think?' Janet's mother replied. 'She popped over a couple of weeks ago, in her reading week – maybe it broke then.'

'I don't know, Mum. She'll be coming home tomorrow and I can ask her then or, better still, why don't you come over for dinner on Sunday and you can bring it with you and show her yourself.'

'What a good idea. It will be lovely to see her – I'll put the chain in an envelope so it doesn't get lost until then.'

Janet put down the phone. Erin must be frantic knowing it was lost – she knew how much the chain meant to her.

Erin just managed to catch the jewellers in town before they shut.

'Can I help you?' The woman behind the counter looked at her watch pointedly.

'I'm looking for a necklace – a gold chain, very fine and about this length.' Erin pointed to her collarbone.

The assistant unlocked one of the glass cabinets and drew out a board of black velvet on which were draped chains in different thicknesses and lengths. Erin picked one out and held it up to her neck. No, the links were too square. The next was too long. The more she looked at the choices, the less able she was to decide which was most like the one her mother had bought her but time was getting on and the assistant was throwing impatient glances at the door. Eventually Erin picked one out.

'I'll take this one,' she said, hoping for the best but as she left the shop and ran her fingers along the length of it, she knew that it wasn't right... it wasn't *her* necklace but maybe her mother wouldn't notice.

Janet had meant to call her daughter to let her know that her grandmother had found her necklace, but it had completely slipped he mind. So when Erin arrived off the train the following weekend, she was surprised to see a fine gold chain around her neck.

As Erin put her bag down in the hall, Janet looked more closely at it: the links seemed a little larger than she remembered and it hung a centimetre below her collarbones. Her hand went to her own necklace and, as it did, she saw he daughter's cheeks colour.

'Is that your necklace, Erin?' she asked.

Her daughter hesitated. 'Yes, of course, Mum. Why do you ask?'

Janet thought of the chain her mother had found. Maybe it wasn't Erin's after all but the chain Erin now wore, she could have sworn was not the same one she had bought her on her eighteenth. 'Oh, no reason,' she said.

When her grandmother arrived the following day, Erin was as pleased as always to see her. As her mother finished preparing the lunch, the two of them sat in the living room and chatted.

'How you've grown, Erin,' her grandmother said, patting her hand.

'It's only two weeks since you've seen me,' Erin laughed, 'and I haven't grown since I was fifteen.'

'Well, you're all grown up and lovely to me, dear. Tell me what you've been doing up at that university of yours. Made any nice friends?'

'Yes, Gran. I've made lots of friends... but I still miss this place.' Without thinking, her hand moved to her neck as it always did when she thought about home. Her grandmother noticed.

'That reminds me, Erin. You didn't lose a necklace did you?' She rummaged in her bag and brought out an envelope. 'I found this down the side of the chair.

I took it the jewellers to see if it could be mended but he said that it would be impossible as it was so fine.'

She tipped the chain into her granddaughter's hand where it lay coiled like a tiny snake.

'Is it yours?'

Erin nodded and her eyes filled at the sight of her beautiful necklace – so precious because her mother had given it to her – but broken now.

'Lunch is ready.' Her mother's voice floated through the open doorway. 'Come and sit down while it's still hot.'

Erin closed her hand over the necklace and looked earnestly at her grandmother.

'Please don't tell her, Gran, about the necklace. I don't want her to know.'

Her grandmother raised her eyebrows. 'Why ever not, dear?'

'I can't ever tell her that I lost it.'

'Erin, your mother...'

But before she could finish her sentence, Erin had slipped the broken chain into her pocket and walked away to the kitchen.

After lunch had finished and Erin was stacking the dishwasher, Janet carried two coffees into the living room. She set one beside her mother then turned and closed the door.

'Mum, you know that necklace you found. Please, whatever you do, don't show it to Erin.'

'And why's that?' her mother asked, taking a sip of the hot drink.

'Because I'm sure the one she's wearing isn't the same one I bought her. I think that she's bought another one so that I won't be angry with her for losing it.'

Her mother's eyes held hers. 'And are you?'

'Of course not. How could you think that?'

'It's not me who thinks it, Janet,' she said.

'But why would she think I'd be angry?'

'Have you thought that it might not be your anger that she's worried about. Since John died, you've been everything to her: Mum, Dad, friend. I expect she just doesn't want to upset you.'

'But it's just a necklace, Mum.'

Her mother raised her hand and touched the fine chain around Janet's neck. 'No, darling, it's much more than that to her.'

The broken chain and the new one that Erin had bought the previous day lay side by side on the coffee table. The three women sat looking at them.

'They are very different, aren't they,' Erin said touching one of the small gold links with her finger. 'I don't know how I thought you wouldn't notice.'

Janet laughed. 'These things happen. I wouldn't have minded... really.'

'But you gave it to me, Mum – that's what made it so special.'

Janet unclasped her own necklace and held it out to Erin. 'Here,' she said. 'I want you to have this one.'

But Erin shook her head. She picked up her own necklace and put it back on.

Janet was about to speak when her mother silenced her.

'I think what Erin's trying to tell you is that she's learnt something important today – something that university could never teach her.' She looked from daughter to granddaughter and smiled.

'We don't need chains to link us together. We are mothers and daughters, and that,' she said taking both their hands, 'is a link that can never be broken.'

CITY SKIES

It was the first week in November and brown and orange leaves still clung to the trees in Patterson Road. For a moment, Katherine felt the usual pleasure at the thought of firework night before remembering: there would be no firework display on the village green this year. For this was not the village of Kettleford, it was London.

Sighing to herself, she put the plastic bag, with its Seven Eleven logo, on the doorstep and reached into her bag for her keys. She tipped her head back and looked at the row of buzzers beside the front door. Next to each one was a plastic holder. She ran a finger down the names: Lorna Buxton, R Hasley, Gina T, Family Kapoor. There were others too but most of them she was unable to read without putting her glasses on.

Half way down, her fingers stopped at an empty holder. She hadn't added her name to the others, although her son Oscar kept saying she should, knowing that if she did, it would mean she would no longer be able to pretend she was just on a weekend break in the city. No, writing her name and slipping it into the little plastic holder would make it real.

Turning her key in the lock, she glanced back down the street. On the opposite side of the road from the tall block of flats that was Harrington Mansions, the red brick Edwardian houses fanned out in a crescent, each one identical to the others. Once, she supposed, they would have belonged to grand families but now they housed a collection of people who barely knew each other. So different from Kettleford. Without warning, a wave of homesickness enveloped her.

She let herself into the bright hallway. At the bottom of the flight of stairs, propped up against the flock wallpaper, was a child's bicycle. It looked like it had seen better days. There were coloured streamers attached to its handlebars and a pink basket on the back. Beside it, was a metal scooter, with most of the paint scratched off, and a pushchair with a pink and white striped seat. Katherine sighed. Her dreams of becoming a grandmother had long ago disappeared – Oscar had made it clear early on that he and Pippa were not planning on having any children.

She held onto the banister and slowly climbed the stairs, preferring it to the lift. Her flat was, after all, only on the second floor and the climb would do her good.

'I hit your green!'

The voice came from the floor above. Resting at the turn of the stairs, she saw a small girl of around seven and a boy who looked slightly older sitting either end of the landing, rolling marbles to one another.

As she passed by, the girl grinned at her, the gap in her front teeth giving her the look of a pirate. She had seen them before, these children, playing in the street outside the flats or bouncing a rubber ball down the steep stairway. At least they were not stuck in front of computers like some of the children in Kettleford.

When the boy jumped up and came towards her, it took her by surprise. He bobbed his dark head at her. 'If you like, I can carry your bag.'

Katherine took a step backwards. She was not used to children talking to her – the Kettleford mothers, with their four by fours and green wellingtons, had drummed it into their little ones that they were, under no circumstances, to talk to strangers. Maybe he wanted to steal it.

'It's quite all right,' she said, holding her bag closer.

'Okay.' The boy looked disappointed and sat back down again.

Almost immediately, Katherine regretted her sharp tone. 'Thank you,' she added.

Feeling a tug on her skirt, she looked down. The little girl grinned at her again, the tip of her tongue poking through the gap in her teeth. Katherine noticed that the end of her long dark plait was wet from where she had been sucking it.

'My name's Badra. It means full moon.'

'Really,' Katherine said. She picked up her bag once more and carried on up the stairs to her own landing. 'That's nice.'

That evening, Oscar rang her. In the flat across the road, a television flickered and she pulled the curtains closed.

'How are you settling in, Mum? We'll come over soon. I promise.'

Katherine looked around her. The flat was nice enough; it was bright and had a cream fitted carpet in all the rooms. It was not her cottage in Kettleford though, with its thatched roof and bow window.

'It's also not damp, Mum, or draughty,' her son said when she told him this. 'And it's near us.'

Katherine had to admit this was true. The windows in the living room were double-glazed and didn't rattle in the wind like her old ones had. Also, despite the large size of the rooms, the central heating was very efficient and of course, Oscar and Pippa were only a ten-minute tube ride away. She held on to this thought – it was the main reason she had decided to move to the city when Terry had died.

'I was wondering,' she said, parting the curtains and watching the wind try to shake the last leaves from the tree in the street below, 'whether you and Pippa might like to come over on bonfire night. I could make some pumpkin soup and we could have some sparklers maybe. It won't be the same as Kettleford but we could pretend.'

Every year, in the village, there would be a big bonfire party on the green. When Oscar was young, she would walk him home from school and each day they would watch the pile of wood grow. When the evening of November the fifth finally arrived, they would stand with their polystyrene cups of soup and gaze into the sky as the fireworks were let off one by one. Even after Oscar had left home and moved to the city, he would return for the celebrations, knowing how much she loved them.

Oscar was speaking again. 'Sorry, Mum. Not this year. Pippa and I are having a few days in Milan – didn't I tell you? Mid-week breaks are cheap at this time of year.'

'No,' Katherine said. 'You didn't say.'

'Look I feel bad now. I know how much you like Bonfire Night. It's just that I thought that now you've moved...'

'It was only a thought, love.' She forced her voice to sound cheerful. Now that she no longer lived in the village, there was no reason why Oscar should still keep up the tradition. Silly of her to imagine he might. 'Don't worry about it. You enjoy your break. You deserve it.'

The next day, Katherine decided to take a bus to the library. She had retired the previous year and, not liking to sit at home twiddling her thumbs, had decided to see what day classes they had in the area.

When she arrived back, her bag stuffed with leaflets, a young woman in a jade green sari, its gold embroidery catching the afternoon sunlight, stood in the hallway. A baby lay in the crook of her arm and she was trying to strap a toddler into the pushchair with the other.

'Can I help?'

The woman looked up at her, through a curtain of shiny black hair. She smiled shyly. 'Thank you.'

Carefully, Katherine took the baby from her. His perfect skin was the colour of a beechnut and he smelt of milk and talcum powder. The baby stared at her with large, dark eyes and for a moment she was transported back to a time, long ago, when Oscar was a baby.

As she watched the woman fasten the straps, the two children Katherine had seen the day before clattered through the door, calling out goodbyes to the mother who had dropped them off. They wore bottle green school uniform and Badra's long dark hair was neatly tied into a plait.

The boy thrust a picture at his mother '*Maa*. I have a painting for you!'

As he pointed to the giant whirls and sprays of colour on the black background, his words ran into one another and Katherine realised he was no longer speaking English.

'Sandeep,' his mother said, stopping him with her hand. 'Where are your manners?'

The boy looked at his feet. 'I am sorry. I'm just excited about bonfire night. We have been learning about Guy Fawkes and how he tried to blow up the Houses of Parliament. Capowwww!'

As the boy made his explosion sound, the baby started and for a moment, Katherine thought he was going to cry. She rocked him gently and soon his eyes started to close again.

'Here,' she said, handing him to Sandeep's mother. 'I think he's nearly asleep.'

The young woman unwound an end of her gauzy sari material and, laying the baby across her chest, wrapped him tightly to her. She bowed her head. 'Thank you. You are very kind.'

Katherine pointed to the colourful drawing in Sandeep's hand. 'It's a very fine picture, young man. The fireworks are just like the ones that we have... use to have... on the village green.'

'Will you see them this year?' The boy asked.

'I'm afraid I won't.' She looked around her. 'This is my home now.'

Turning sadly away, she left the young family to collect their scooters and bicycles – their happy chatter echoing in the hallway.

November the fifth dawned crisp and clear. Katherine had planned to spend the day unpacking the remaining boxes that stood unopened in the second bedroom but when it came to it, she found that something would always stop her: a change of address to be made or a request to be put on the register at the doctor's surgery.

It wasn't until lunchtime, when she opened her fridge, that she realised she hadn't any milk. It was a good job the Seven Eleven was just a street away. Putting on her coat, she walked down the two flights of stairs and stepped out onto Patterson Road. The wind was brisk and as she walked, the yellow and orange leaves rose up from the pavement in little flurries.

There weren't many people in the shop, just a few office workers buying a quick sandwich. When she got to the till, she placed her few items on the counter. The man at the till raised his head and when he saw her, a smile lit up his face.

'It is very good to see you!'

Sure that she had not seen him before, Katherine hesitated. The middle-aged man's thick hair was oiled to a shine and his belly, covered in a white collarless shirt, embroidered down the front in an intricate design, rested on the counter.

'It is Mr Kapoor. We live on the top floor of Harrington Mansions. My children have spoken of you.'

Katherine thought of the beautiful young woman she had met earlier that week and was surprised. She must be his wife.

'I met your family only the other day. You have a lovely baby.'

Mr Kapoor beamed and puffed himself up. 'I am very proud. Very proud indeed.'

Katherine paid for her shopping and had just turned to leave when Mr Kapoor called after her. 'We would be very honoured if you would be our guest this evening. The children would be very happy to see you.'

Katherine was taken aback but then she thought of Oscar and Pippa, at that moment flying to their hotel in Milan. It might not be her usual Bonfire Night, but at least it would be company.

'Thank you,' she said. 'I would like that very much.'

Katherine took the lift to the fourth floor. As she stepped out onto the landing, a wonderful smell met her. Not the usual bonfire night smell of jacket potatoes or pumpkin soup but something warmer... spicier.

Before she could knock on the door, it burst open and the children tumbled out. Sandeep was dressed in royal blue loose-fitting trousers and an embroidered tunic and Badra's jade sari was a miniature version of the one her mother had been wearing when Katherine had last seen her.

'We've been waiting for you.'

The children took her by the hands and pulled her through the front door. It led straight into a large living area. There were two settees draped with red embroidered throws and, between them, a carved coffee table covered with Lego. On the walls, posters of temples and prints of elephants fought for space with the children's artwork.

The children settled themselves cross-legged on the floor with a pack of cards and Katherine wondered where to sit; the settees were strewn with baby paraphernalia and colourful magazines. She was just moving the baby's mosses basket onto the floor to make room to sit down when Mr Kapoor came into the room, a striped apron around his ample middle.

'My wife will be with you soon. She is just putting the little one to bed. I, as you can see,' he said grinning from ear to ear, 'am making our bonfire night feast!'

The delicious smell that had permeated the landing was stronger now and Katherine found her mouth watering. In the kitchen behind Mr Kapoor, she could see a selection of pans on the stove, their lids rattling as fragrant steam escaped from them. On the kitchen table, metal dishes with handles stood waiting.

'Is there anything I can do to help?' she asked.

'No, no!' Mr Kapoor looked shocked. 'You are our guest, Mrs Edwards.'

He lifted his apron and dabbed at the perspiration on his brow. 'You like curry?'

Katherine thought of the rather insipid coconut dishes her husband used to choose for them both or the fiery Vindaloos that her son favoured. She'd tried some once and it wasn't an experience she wished to repeat.

Mr Kapoor was looking at her expectantly.

'I am sure I shall find it... lovely.'

The man grinned and nodded so hard his jowls wobbled. 'Very good. Very good.'

'It is nice of you to come.' Mrs Kapoor stood in the doorway, her beautiful face serene. Her hair was twisted into a bun and where it had been pulled back, it shone like a raven's wing. The baby lay asleep across one arm and with the other she adjusted the folds of her pale blue sari.

'Would you mind?' She stepped forwards and handed the baby to Katherine before disappearing into the kitchen with her husband.

Katherine watched the children playing with the cards – a shout of, *Snap!* coming from them every so often and as she sung to the baby a song that she had sung to her own boy, she found that she was feeling more relaxed than she had for many months.

Soon, Mrs Kapoor came back into the room, a bowl of steaming rice in her hands. Behind her, her husband carried a large tray full of dishes. He pushed the Lego off the coffee table with the end of the tray and proceeded to place the bowls in front of her, pointing to each one in turn.

'Dal makhani... palak paneer... biriani...' He lifted a plate of deep fried pastry triangles. 'Try a samosa, Mrs Edwards. You will find them most pleasing.'

'Please, call me Katherine.'

Mrs Kapoor took the baby from her and she took a samosa from the offered plate. She bit into it; the filling was spicy and delicious.

'These are very good, Mr Kapoor.'

'Rashi,' he beamed. 'And my wife is Rupi – it means beauty... very fitting don't you think?'

As he looked at his wife, the young woman smiled and bowed her head. 'Children,' she said. 'Come and join us or the food will get cold.'

They all crowded around the wooden table and as Katherine tried each fragrant dish, she realised that in all the years she had lived in Kettleworth, she had never encountered such warmth and hospitality – and from virtual strangers too.

She looked at her empty plate, dabbing her mouth with her serviette. She smiled at the family gathered around her. 'It has all been quite delicious but I mustn't outstay my welcome. I am sure you have things to do.'

She would go back to her flat – maybe look at old photographs of the bonfire nights on Kettleworth Green. Or maybe she wouldn't. Outside, in the distance, she could hear whizzes and bangs – despite the lovely evening she had had, she missed the country village and the fireworks lighting up the sky.

'Don't go, Mrs Edwards!' the children chorused.

'The children are right.' Rashi stood and walked to the window where red hessian curtains hung down to the floor. He pulled them back to reveal French doors that opened onto a small balcony.

He held out his hand. 'Come see.'

Katherine took a step out onto the balcony, followed by Rupi and the children. Below her, the streets of the city spread out, row upon row. Ribbons of headlights from cars, which looked as small as the toy ones Oscar used to play with, weaved their way between the twinkling lights of the buildings. But it was not this that made her gasp... for across the night sky, something wonderful was happening.

All across the city, fireworks were exploding. Whichever way she looked, sparkling trails of light burst into glittering circles. The bangs and crackles she had heard earlier were louder now, heralding new displays above the rooftops.

'Look,' Sandeep cried, pointing to the west where the distant Thames snaked its way through the city. Each explosion of colour was reflected in the ribbon of water, like a thousand starbursts.

Rashi stood with his hands on his hips, a satisfied look on his face. 'My son said you sounded sad when you talked about the fireworks in the village where you lived. We wanted to show you that we have fireworks in the city too – it was Sandeep's idea. It is to welcome you.'

Katherine thought of the cards lined up on her coffee table and the flowers in vases. 'I think this is the best housewarming present I could wish for.'

'We hope you will be very happy here in Patterson Road.'

Katherine gazed across the city. She had moved to London to be near her son but he had his own life to lead and so did she. She thought of her modern flat, her newfound friends and all the new experiences that awaited her outside the front door of Harrington Mansions. Tomorrow she would unpack the last of the boxes.

'Do you know something, Rashi?' she said, a delicious feeling of anticipation stirring inside her. 'I think I shall.'

THE WRITING ON THE WALL

The word appears slowly. As I pull away wet strips of wallpaper, the wall beneath is slick and shiny with paste but with every upward sweep of the scraper, the letters become more defined. Some letters are written large and others smaller. The writing is bold and defiant, written across the blank canvas of the wall with a flourish. The light is going and dusk has fallen by the time I uncover the final letter.

REMEMBER

Remember what?

I remember seeing this house for the first time. I was twenty-two. The sky hung low and grey and the rain lashed at the windows, obliterating any view there might have been from upstairs. My husband of two months had hung around on the landing, furling his umbrella and shifting his weight from one shiny brogue to the other.

'Are there any more houses we can look at before it gets dark?' His voice sounded strange in the empty shell of the house.

There had been more but none like this. This house sang out to me from the deluge and I remember feeling this was what it must be like to be Noah on his ark. The new life within me softly stirred and I stroked promises to it through my taut skin.

Although I have lived in this house for thirty years, it is the first time I have felt ready to remove the wallpaper so carefully chosen that springtime as I was preparing for motherhood.

The room is small, oblong, ordinary even and has been neglected over the years. It is neither a catcher of the early morning sun nor a keeper of its final rays, due to its northerly direction. It contains a small desk by the patio doors and a book case full to overflowing – both now covered in a dustsheet.

I look at the wall. The single word looks unfinished. There is more – I know there is more. I take up the scraper again and attack the wall with an energy that I do not understand or recognise in myself. More letters take shape.

REMEMBER THIS

My mother used to catch me by the hand as I went out to play on a Saturday morning.

'Remember this,' she would say, curling my fingers around a half crown. 'You can't buy happiness but you can buy an ice cream.'

I smile at the memory. My mother in her quilted dressing gown, waving from the half open door – how embarrassed I had been in case she was seen by my friends. The coin safely in my pocket, I would run across to my friend Pam's house and the normality of a mother who started her morning in slacks.

My mother lives alone, like me. We have both had disappointments in our lives. She collects shells and driftwood from the beach near her bungalow. Spiky hatpins crowned with pearls and beaded clusters are stuck into faded velvet pincushions on top of bookshelves. A glass cabinet sports china shoes, stamped with coats of arms and the names of seaside towns.

'I remember this,' I sometimes say to her, turning the cool china in my hand. My mother remembers with me but sometimes forgets to empty the bin or turn off the gas.

I put down the scraper and pick up my mobile instead.

'Hello, Mum. How's things? Yes I'm fine – just stripping some wallpaper and I got to thinking that I haven't seen you for a while. How about some lunch tomorrow? No, no, of course I haven't better things to be doing. The wall can wait.'

The wall remains as it is for another day. After seeing my mother, I peep into the room as if to see if something has changed but the words stare back at me – a command or a question. I am in no mood for its words and its secrets – preferring sleep.

The clock shows three in the morning. The bedclothes are twisted and damp and my throat is dry. I walk down the stairs and towards the kitchen for some water. I glance into the room. A neon streetlight filters through the venetian blinds and throws horizontal white bars across the wall as if to underline the words written there. I cannot help myself. I plunge my hand, with its sponge, into the large bowl of water that I have left on the floor and squeeze it onto the wallpaper.

Taking the scraper, I catch the edge of the paper and force the metal down between the slippery back and the bare plaster.

REMEMBER THIS ROOM

A long strip of paper hangs down almost to the floor. Monkeys swing from palms and fat hippos sit next to placid lions. The cot had been here, over in this corner. I can still feel the downy head with its sweet powdery smell resting in the crook of my arm. Hours spent in this room, wishing for sleep, for his sleep, for mine.

The paper never changed but the bed became a single and then a bunk. Rattles and soft toys were replaced with cars and transformers, then Xboxes and computers. The monkeys and lions were covered with posters of Madonna and U2. Shoes got bigger; cups and mugs were left to fester under piles of underwear. First one son and then the other found work and wives and their own lives. I remember this was a happy room. It deserves to be a happy room again.

I know there is more. I can feel it calling to be released from its papery imprisonment. This time I scrape slowly. I savour each scrape, pulling the strips away like the bark from a tree.

There – it it done. It is a surprise and not a surprise.

REMEMBER THIS ROOM IS SPECIAL

I sit on the floor and laugh until I cry. I know now whose hand crafted these long forgotten words. How was it that I forgot? I sit with my back against the monkeys and lions and with closed eyes replay the memory like a silent movie. I watch myself, as a young woman, slant my hidden message of hope to my unborn son. A talisman – long forgotten but there all the same.

This room may not see the early morning light but its restful tones aid my thoughts and its memories feed my imagination. It contains my desk and my bookcase and the ghosts of my life. The stories I create on my computer are written to celebrate a life both past and yet to be lived. There is nothing grand about this room but it is my room now and I will remember that this room was, and always will be, special.

FEELS LIKE COMING HOME

Amelia parked the hire car outside the newsagents at the end of the road and waited for her heart to stop thumping. Pulling down the sun visor, she squinted into the mirror and reapplied some lipstick – putting off the moment when she would have to face her family. The black sheep.

The nine-hour flight from Nashville had tired her and she longed for the softness of her childhood bed but that wouldn't be possible unless she walked down the front path and rang on the doorbell. She imagined the scene that awaited her at number 33 Cherry Tree Close. She pictured her mother walking to the window and pulling back the yellowing nets, the better to catch a first glimpse of her eldest daughter. She would look back at her grandfather, who had moved in after Grandma Livy had died, and shake her head and together, in hushed tones, they would discuss the day she had left.

Amelia's thoughts moved on to Chrissie. What would her younger sister be doing? She felt the usual stab of guilt. How long was it since she had last seen her – two years... three? Would she have changed? She wondered whether her auburn hair still framed her heart shaped face or if she tied it back now and if she still favoured the thin beaded bracelets that crept up her arm.

Playing for time, Amelia let herself out of the car and walked towards the newsagents. She'd buy a magazine or something. Anything to put off the moment when she would have to meet her family again.

The assistant was restocking the magazine shelf. She looked up as the door tinkled.

'Won't be a minute,' she said, bending to pick up the last two celebrity magazines and placing them on the stand with the others. The smiling face of a woman, her strawberry blond curls falling over her shoulders, stared out from the front cover. *Country singer, Amelia Lang, talks about her tour.*

Amelia turned her head away, letting her hair swing across her face in an effort to hide it. She placed a newspaper on the counter along with the correct change, hoping she could leave without having to have the inevitable conversation. But the assistant was already staring at her with the awestruck expression that Amelia had come to recognise wherever she went. Ordinarily, she relished the attention and the chance to talk to her fans but not here – not in her hometown.

'I'll just take these. I think you'll find that's the correct money.'

The assistant nodded and put the money in the till but Amelia knew that she was finding it hard not to stare. As soon as she had left, she would be texting someone to tell them that Amelia Lang, of all people, had been in her shop. Taking a deep breath, she forced a smile. 'Thank you.'

As she walked back out onto the street, a poster in the window caught her eye.

Crazy Catz Bar and Bistro
Tuesday's Country Nite!
Chrissie Lang

She stopped and pressed her finger against the glass and drew it across her sister's name. Three years ago, the words would have said *Amelia and Chrissie Lang*. That was until she had made the choice... the choice that was to change her life forever.

She closed her eyes and rested her forehead against the cold window as the memory of that evening flooded back.

The guy on the barstool was someone important. She could sense it. The way he spoke into his mobile and the way he wore his clothes. *Artfully casual* Chrissie would have called it, if she had been there, but that day she wasn't. The sore throat that had been plaguing her for the last few days had got worse and tonight Amelia was going to be singing alone.

The crowd was a good one. Buzzing. Most of the tables were filled and the opening band had gone down well. The early customers, who had come to eat, had finished and their places at the white Formica tables were being taken by the late evening crowd.

Amelia sat at the other end of the bar from the stranger, tuning her guitar – she'd be on in a minute. She leant across the bar and caught the owner's eye.

'Who's that guy?'

'He's American,' Cat said. 'Heard they've sent someone across the pond from John Castle Music... they're looking for something new. Likes the idea of a Brit. It could be your lucky night.'

Amelia felt her heart beat faster. 'How long's he here for?'

'Just the night, I think, then a couple of nights in London before moving up North.'

'I can't believe he's here.' Amelia watched the man's slim fingers lift his pint glass. 'What made him come to this little place?'

'Tip off. Someone said our country night was the best in the South and it might be worth him taking a look. Never had a talent scout here before. It'll be good for custom.'

And maybe for me. How long had she dreamed of something like this happening? Amelia ran her fingers through her hair to loosen the curls and then slid off the stool. She walked to the back of the bar and stepped onto the stage. As she stroked a chord, the voices in the room quietened – all eyes turned to her. They were regulars and she knew that, even without Chrissie there, they would be appreciative.

'I'm going to start with an old favourite to get you in the mood. This one's called Take Me Home Country Roads. I'm sure you'll all know it and, if you do, why don't y'all join in.'

It seemed strange not having Chrissie beside her as she sang. She was used to her gentle harmonies and the soft rasp of the harmonica. But soon the music took her over and she forgot about her sister. As she sang, she closed her eyes and let her head nod forward in time with the music – her hair falling in curtains across her face.

She played an old song by Patsy Cline – one her grandmother loved – and then some more up-tempo numbers and when she at last raised her head, acknowledging the applause, she was aware of the man's eyes fixed on her. Raising her hand in thanks, she lifted the guitar over her head, leant it against the wall and walked to the bar.

'Nice set.' The man at the bar held out his hand. 'I'm Max. Hi.'

Amelia turned to him and smiled. 'My grandmother told me never to use the word *nice*. Said that it tells you nothing of interest.'

'Hmm. Wise words. Here's to your grandmother.' He raised his glass. 'You've got a good... no, sorry... unique voice. We're looking for new solo country artists and you might be just what we're looking for.'

Amelia felt her heart flutter with excitement and in that moment all thoughts of Chrissie were forgotten. 'Really?'

'Just one thing though. Do you have any of your own material? I'd like to hear you do something fresher... more contemporary. Got anything?'

Amelia thought for a moment. There was that song – the one that Chrissie had written in their shared bedroom. She pictured her sister cross-legged on the flowered quilt, her head bowed over a music score and a pencil between her teeth as she hummed out the melody. The previous week, they had tried it out – their hands strumming their guitars in unison and their voices blending.

'There is one...'

'Good. Let's hear it then.'

Amelia went back to her stool and picked up her guitar again. Chrissie wouldn't mind her using her song, surely. She strummed the first chord and as she started to sing, the air in the bar became electric and she was soon lost in the music.

Whenever I'm with you... Feels like coming home

At the end of the evening, John handed her his card. 'A talented singer and song writer,' he said. 'Just what we're looking for – you'll be hearing from me.'

'Excuse me.'

Amelia opened her eyes, aware that she was blocking the cards in the newsagent's window.

'Sorry.' She stepped away from the glass and started her walk down Cherry Tree Close. She would have to face her family sooner or later.

At the first knock, the front door flew open.

'Darling!' Amelia's mother pulled her into her arms and then stood back to look at her. She touched the fur collar of her coat. 'Just look at you. You've done so well for yourself.'

Amelia shrugged off the coat and hung it on the hat stand in the hallway. 'It's nothing, Mum. It doesn't even keep out the cold.'

'Well, let's not just stand in the doorway. Grandad's been like a cat on a hot tin roof waiting for you to arrive. You'll be a comfort to him now you're here.'

Again, she felt the wash of guilt as she pushed open the door to the sitting room and saw her dear grandfather in his chair – a scrapbook on his lap. As he struggled to his feet, she hurried to stop him.

'Don't get up, Grandad.'

She sat down on the arm of his chair, noticing that his bald spot was more pronounced than before.

'I'm sorry about Grandma Livy. I would have come sooner but...'

Her grandfather patted her hand. 'Don't worry, Pet. Your mum told me all about the tour. I know how important it was.'

'But I missed the funeral, Grandad.'

'Liv wouldn't have minded – probably would have done the same thing in your shoes. She was proud of you, love. Told everyone at bingo that her granddaughter was a big country star. Kept all your clippings in this scrapbook. Did you know that?'

Amelia shook her head, her eyes prickling. If she had only been in contact more, she might have known these things.

'You look beautiful, love,' he said, fingering her blond curls. 'Success suits you.'

Amelia looked at the floor. 'I'm sorry I haven't been home much. There's been the album and then the tour and...'

'You don't have to explain. We're all just happy to see your lovely face.'

Her mother pushed open the door, a tray of cups in her hands. 'I've brought some tea. How are you feeling, dear? You can have a nap later if you want – your old room's ready for you.'

Amelia stood awkwardly. 'I'm all right at the moment, Mum. Where's Chrissie?'

'She'll be here soon. She's just finishing her shift at the care home. She'll be pleased to see you.'

Amelia closed her eyes for a moment, letting her mother's words settle around her. Why couldn't they all be honest – admit the hurt and the disappointment that they felt, rather than keeping up this charade of being happy at her homecoming. She walked to the window, propping her elbows on the sill and looking out onto the garden where she and Chrissie had played when they were small. The late afternoon sun was casting long stripes of shadow across the lawn.

'You haven't drunk your tea. Maybe you'd prefer a piece of lemon drizzle – I made it this morning.'

Amelia turned. The room suddenly felt too warm, too small to contain all the emotions that she knew were fighting for space within its four walls. She could stand it no longer.

'I need some air, Mum,' she said.

Her mother raised her eyebrows in surprise. 'But you just got here, darling.'

'I know, sorry. I won't be long. I'll just take the path to Galley Hill – it'll clear my head from the flight.'

'Amelia... wait!' The voice was small, distant.

Below her, the figure picked its way between the heather and gorse bushes. She could tell it was Chrissie by the bow of her head and the determined way she was climbing the hill.

The evening sky had started to stretch its orange fingers towards the horizon and Amelia shivered. She wrapped her arms around her body and waited for Chrissie to catch up. What would she say to her? Could she explain?

How they had loved this place, she and Chrissie. As teenagers, while their friends were hanging around the arcades or swimming at the sports centre, she and her sister would take their guitars up to the top of

Galley Hill. They would sit cross-legged on the short turf and sing, all the while looking down at the town and the slow moving river. She remembered the flat round thistles that looked like buttons set into upholstery and the prickle of the grass on the back of her legs.

Here, on this hill, they had sung the songs by Patsy Cline and Loretta Lynn so loved by their grandmother and talked of one day becoming country stars. By the time they had left school, they had got themselves a regular slot at Crazy Catz, playing for beer money. *Tuesday's Country Nite!* She remembered the way their voices had harmonised when they sang their usual encore of *Country Roads*.

'This climb doesn't get any easier, does it?' Chrissie bent at the waist with her hands on her knees, her breath coming in gasps. After a while, her breathing became easier. She stood and looked out over the town.

'I still come here, you know. When I want to get inspiration.'

'I miss it,' Amelia said, glad to be talking about ordinary things. 'How's Gary?'

Her sister's face lit. 'He's good.'

Amelia shifted her feet and stared out towards the town, now silhouetted against the orange sky. 'And your job? Is it going well?'

'I love it. They're making me assistant manager soon.' Her sister turned and looked at her. 'Look, when did we become such strangers?'

Amelia remained silent. *Since I stole your dream.*

'You don't phone, you don't email.' Chrissie placed her hand on Amelia's arm. 'Everyone's so proud of you.'

Amelia turned round. Her voice was strained. 'Look, stop pretending. It's bad enough Mum and Grandad making out that nothing's wrong, but I can't bare it from you.'

Chrissie took a step towards her. 'I don't know what you mean. We just want you to be happy. You are, aren't you?'

Was she? She loved the music, the excitement of playing before an audience in a big stadium and the thrill when she heard her own voice singing the songs she loved on the radio. She should have been happy but something stopped her and it was time to face it. Time to tell the truth.

'I'm sorry, Chrissie,' she said.

Her sister's face was puzzled. 'What for?'

She knew she had to tell her – it was eating away at her. She took a deep breath. 'That night when Max Joyce heard me sing at Crazy Catz, I told him that your song *Feels Like Coming Home* was my own. He loved it. I think it's what made up his mind. I wanted to tell you when I got home... but I couldn't. I didn't know how.'

The two sisters stood silent for a moment, the only sound the rooks in the trees settling for the night.

'He wanted to put it on the album but I wouldn't let him. It felt wrong... say something, please, Chrissie.'

It was a moment before she realised that her sister was laughing softly. 'Is that the reason why we don't hear from you... because of me?'

'Do you hate me?'

Chrissie sat on the short grass and indicated for Amelia to do likewise. 'Don't you know me at all? I never would have wanted to go. Don't get me wrong – I love singing at Catz on a Tuesday night but that's the extent of it. My life is here... with Gary.'

'But we dreamed of...'

'No, Amelia, you did. It was never my dream. You always had the drive and the ambition. I was happy just to sing with you, just like we always did at Grandad and Grandma Liv's, when we played her old records. I never wanted more than that.'

'But I stole your song!'

'You can't steal something that's yours. I wrote that song for you... have you never listened to the words?'

She sang softly to herself. *'Ties like this can't be broken. Go where life wants you, I'll be here waiting till you call.'*

'I've been so stupid.'

A narrow crescent of moon could just be seen between the branches of the trees and the track up the hill was becoming indistinct.

'We'd better be getting back,' Chrissie said. 'Mum will be getting worried. But promise me one thing, Amelia – that you'll come to Crazy Catz and sing with me tonight.'

Amelia smiled and for the first time in three years the knot in her stomach loosened. 'There's nothing I'd like more.'

The white tables were filling up and the country band before them was just leaving the small stage.

'We're next,' Chrissie said. 'Nervous?'

Amelia laughed. 'As I've ever been.'

'Wait here a moment.' Chrissie stepped onto the stage and lifted her guitar over her head – adjusting the strap. She looked out across the tables.

'Good to see you all. Tonight though, I won't be singing on my own. I have someone very special who will be joining me... Ladies and gentlemen, let me introduce Amelia Lang. My sister.'

As Amelia joined Chrissie on the stage, she heard the surprised gasps from the audience. She took the guitar that Chrissie handed to her and as she did, she saw her mother and grandfather slip in at the back of the room.

'Hi everyone,' she said. 'Tonight I am privileged to be singing with my sister Chrissie. I'm sure you will all agree you are very lucky to have her here at Crazy Catz. The first song we would like to sing tonight is one that will be featuring on my new album. It was written by Chrissie and we hope y'all like it.'

She waved to her family at the back of the room. 'It's good to be back. Grandad... this one's for Grandma Liv.'

As one, the sisters strummed their guitars and the room fell silent as they started singing.

Whenever I'm with you... feels like coming home.

ALL OUR YESTERDAYS

My stomach does a flip as the basket leaves the ground. It is early and the sun has only just risen above the brow of the hill. All around us, the glow of burners can be seen filling the candy striped balloons that scatter the field.

Kieran was right; it's going to be a lovely day – only a few puffy clouds disturbing the ice blue of the sky. He has spent days scouring the forecasts and speaking with his ballooning friends – just to make sure that everything will be perfect. Only for me, the day's beauty has no meaning. This day, like all the others, will be long and grey.

'Hold tight, Jude.'

The burner breathes a hot gasp of air into the balloon and the basket rises steadily. I grip its wicker edge, unsure of why I have agreed to come on this trip. I think it must have been Mum's worried face... or maybe Kieran's. They only want the best for me, I know that, but they don't know what it feels like to be me. To be in my body. Knowing that nothing will ever be the same again.

I look up at Kieran's face. His strong chin is raised and the brown curls, that I love so much, blow away from his brow in the increasing breeze. He is concentrating hard; staring at the altimeter as we rise higher. He sees me looking and strokes my hair away from my face. 'Look down, Jude. Tell me what you see.'

I clutch at the edge of the basket and pull myself unsteadily to my feet. Below us, the fields are reduced to a patchwork blanket.

'Nothing. Just fields.'

'Look closer. Our house must be down there somewhere.'

Doesn't he realise that I don't want to see the house – its four walls like a prison to me?

'I'll take her down lower. Look, there it is across the other side of the road.'

A small figure stands in the garden, hand shielding her eyes as she stares up into the sky. It's Mum – a small pushchair parked next to her.

I turn away but cannot hide the pain in my heart. Kieran sees. He tries a smile.

'There's Simian. Over there by the fence.' The stallion dips his head before trotting along the edge of the field. 'Looks like he's enjoying the sunshine.'

My voice wavers. 'Why are you doing this, Kieran?'

'Because it's not Simian's fault, Jude... it's no one's fault.'

I know it's true. Simian didn't ask for the dog to bark just as we were entering the lane behind the stables. He was scared. I know that.

The balloon glides effortlessly through the sky. I am surprised that I am not more nervous but then maybe I shouldn't be surprised. After all, I used to be fearless. The taker of chances.

'Remember when we borrowed some skates and went out onto the lake, that winter? I think it was 98.' It is as if he has read my thoughts. 'Foolish weren't we... but it wasn't half fun. There it is down there.'

The lake glints in the sunlight, a mirror of blue. I feel again the cold nip of winter on my cheek and Kieran's warm hand in mine as he leads me onto the ice.

'We made sure we were only a foot away from the edge just in case.'

I can't help smiling. 'Not so brave after all.'

Kieran pulls on the cord in his hand, opening the valve and letting some hot air escape. The patchwork of fields grows bigger. 'There's St. Katherine's. That was probably the bravest thing you ever did... marrying me.' He strokes my cheek. 'It will be five years tomorrow.'

I know that of course. It's just that I had been hoping that Kieran had forgotten. I'm not the same girl he married. Can never be. I've let him down.

'It was a beautiful day. You were the most beautiful girl in Stanbury.' He gazes down at the little church. 'I thought I was the luckiest man alive when you said, *I do*. I still think that, Jude.'

I pretend not to hear but look at the little unkempt graveyard, its grey headstones like sharp rocks in a wild green sea, and remember how the future shone so brightly ahead of us that day.

'Yes,' I say. 'It was a beautiful day.'

'And remember when Candy had her christening there, how she threw up over the vicar's shoes!'

My heart aches at the thought of my child. For the first time in three months I want to hold her in my arms and I wish she was up here with us to share our beautiful world in the sky.

A blue and white balloon sails away ahead of us. I am starting to understand why Kieran loves this so much. Everything is so peaceful up here. I feel free.

Kieran stands behind me, supporting me as I lean over the side. 'There's the village hall where we danced to Phil Collins... oh, what was the song?'

'Can't Stop Lovin' You,' I say, and I remember the feel of his arms around me. 'We were eighteen. There's the oak where we carved our names...'

'And where I asked you to marry me.'

I close my eyes and remember. 'I've been a cow, haven't I... these last three months?'

'No one can blame you for the way you've been feeling, Jude. It's been a tough time – we've all had to make adjustments. You, me, your mum... even Candy.'

'I just feel so useless, Kieran. Not being able to take her to nursery, or carry her up to bed.' I feel the tears prick the back of my eyes.

Kieran opens the propane valve to let the flame burn brighter in the balloon and we rise once more over the village until it looks like a scene from a children's book. He leans back into me again, his face against mine.

'These are our yesterdays,' he says sweeping a hand across the chequered landscape. 'Some good, some great and some we wished hadn't happened, but do you know what?'

I turn and look into his brown eyes. 'What?'

'Those yesterdays are what have made us who we are today. When I met you, you were fearless – that's what I loved most about you.' He places a gentle hand over the slight swell of my belly. 'You're still that same person, Jude. Nothing can change that. You were brave before the accident and you can be brave again.'

'I'm scared, Kieran.'

'I know you are but you were... are... a fantastic mother to Candy and you will be to her little brother or sister.'

I place my hand over his and feel my body move gently under our touch.

'You won't be on your own, Jude. There'll be me and your mother to help.'

I know he's right. Below us, in the car park next to the field I see our Land Rover, my wheelchair folded in the boot, but for the first time in a long while I feel a stir of excitement about the future.

As the balloon slowly descends, I take a last look across the landscape that has shaped my life.

From the wicker basket, I may have seen all our yesterdays mapped out in the contours of the land and the geometry of the buildings but I have also seen the promise of a brave new future.

With a soft thud, we land and Kieran gently lifts me out of the basket. I smile at him. 'Let's go home,' I say.

A GROWING FAMILY

'Come and stand by the door, John. Let's see how much you've grown since last time.'

Thelma stood in the open doorway to the living room, peering at a column of horizontal pen marks that could just be seen on the inside of the doorframe. She waited as her grandson navigated the small space between the coffee table, on which was spread the pieces of a puzzle, and his toolbox which he'd left in the middle of the floor. She was pleased that he had suggested braving the South Circular to look at her leaky radiator; that plumbing course he had started was certainly coming in handy.

'Haven't you finished that puzzle yet, Nan? I'm sure you were doing it last time I was here.' John joined her in the doorway and obediently stood with his back flat against the doorframe.

'Oh, that would have been the first time. I've done it a few times since then.' Thelma moved John to one side to centre him against the wood. 'It's no good. I'm going to have to get a chair.'

'Let me get it, Nan.'

'Don't be silly. I'm perfectly capable.' She went into the kitchen and reappeared a few minutes later with a chair which she dragged up against the frame.

'I really don't think you should be climbing on that.'

Thelma tutted. 'Well I can hardly ask you to bend your knees can I? That would rather defeat the object.'

She took John's offered hand and climbed onto the chair, steadying herself with one hand on the doorframe as she straightened up. 'Now pass me the Enid Blyton.'

John chuckled. 'Same old book, Nan.'

'Of course. I wouldn't use anything else. Now hold your head straight.' She lifted his chin a fraction and placed the book flat on the top of his head before making a new mark with the pen. 'Still growing, I see.'

Placing her hand on John's shoulder, Thelma lowered herself back onto the floor and stood in front of the doorframe. What a fine young man he's turned into, she thought. She took her glasses from where they were hanging from a cord around her neck, and peered at the marks that she had made over the years.

'Difficult to believe you were only that high once,' she said, indicating a mark near the bottom. She bent a little closer, smiling to herself at the memory of the six-year-old John wriggling against the doorframe. Just like me at the same age, she thought, straightening up then standing on tiptoe. 'And look, that was your dad at nineteen. You've got a couple of inches on him.'

'Yeah,' John laughed, 'and doesn't he just hate it.'

As they sat back down in the living room, Thelma noticed her grandson glance over at the letter on the sideboard.

'Have you made a decision yet, Nan?'

'So your father sent you. It wasn't just the radiator then?' Thelma's tone was sharp and John flinched.

'No.' Despite Thelma's wish to believe him, John had never been a good liar.

'I'm not going, you know. I've lived here all my life.' She picked up a piece of puzzle which had been put in the wrong place and stared at it. *That's what they'd like to do to me,* she thought.

'But Nan, the council say these houses…'

'There's nothing wrong with these houses – solid as rocks. Saw out the blitz, which is more than I can say for some.' The memory had not faded over the decades.

'Come on Thelma, it's safe to come out now.' The all clear wailed its banshee note and a six-year-old Thelma peeked out from beneath the lace edge of the tablecloth. They had heard the drone of the planes almost as soon as the air raid siren had started and Thelma's mother had taken her hand and led her to the back door.

'I don't want to go!' Thelma had pulled and squirmed and cried herself hoarse until, in desperation, her mother had decided that maybe the dining room table was a better option. As they huddled together, Thelma was glad, despite the distant rumblings of the bombs, that they had not gone out across the dark back garden to the Anderson shelter. How she hated it with its damp smell and spidery darkness, broken only by the dim glow of an oil lamp.

Now, she felt her mother pick her up, smoothing her hair from her damp cheeks. 'What a fuss, Thelma. My, but you're getting to be such a big girl. I swear you've grown another inch in the last week and how you manage that on these rations is beyond me.' She put Thelma down and steered her to the doorway that led into the hall. 'Here, stand against this and we'll see how big you've got.'

Thelma drew herself up as tall as she could as she felt the downward pressure of a book being placed on her head. 'Stop moving about, Thelma. You're as wriggly as a puppy.'

She watched as her mother marked the frame and placed the book back on the arm of the chair – *Five on a Treasure Island*. Although she couldn't read that well yet, she had spent many hours staring longingly at the cover.

Now, as she looked at the picture of the children, carefree and windswept, sailing off on their adventure, she thought about her father. Her mother had said that he was off on an adventure too but it had been a long time since he had last been home and the thought of him made her sad. Sometimes she worried that she was starting to forget his face and when this happened, she would run up the stairs, stand on tiptoe in front of her mother's dressing table and gaze at his photograph in its gilt frame.

'Look,' her mother said now. 'Look how tall you are. You take after your Daddy.'

Thelma lifted her head until she could see the mark her mother had made on the doorframe the last time her father had been home. As her mother had balanced the book on his head, he had kissed her and laid his hand on her rounded tummy.

'That's your little sister or brother,' he had said, turning to her with a wink. 'Wonder if the new one will be as stubborn as you!'

Her father's voice merged with John's. 'The houses are in a poor state of repair and suffer from many of the problems associated with pre-war housing including poor insulation, poor access and parking arrangements and management and maintenance difficulties...'

Thelma opened her eyes to see her grandson reading aloud from the letter. He was a good boy – like his dad and his grandfather before him. Thoughtful and kind. *With none of your stubbornness*, her husband had liked to joke.

John looked a lot like his grandfather she thought and, although she tried to block it out, what he was reading struck a chord. Although she would admit it to nobody, the house was becoming a problem. She hated the way the damp got into her bones and how the rooms never seemed to warm up despite the heating being turned up high. At night, she would lie awake listening to the rattle of the sash windows and long for warmth and comfort.

'It can't be much fun for you here, now that most of your neighbours have gone,' John said, putting his arm around her. 'Things around here have changed, Nan.'

She knew this: Marleen next door had sold to the council and moved to Green Acres, *the modern estate with its proximity to local services and green spaces,* as soon as the first letter had arrived and one by one her other neighbours had followed. Fine if you liked living in a maze.

'Your father was born in this house, John.' The story was not new to her grandson but Thelma felt a great need to tell him again.

'I think they've started.'

Thelma's mother smiled at her and rubbed her back. 'I think you're right, we'd better phone the midwife – second babies are always quicker.'

Thelma looked at her husband who was standing in the doorway, a look of concern on his face. 'Why don't you and Dad go to the pub for a bit? There's nothing you can do here.' She winced as another pain built up.

'Don't you think you should be having the baby in the hospital, Thelma, like Marleen did next door? The doctor said it's the safest way.'

'We've talked about this before. I'm not going. This is the nineteen sixties and I can have my baby where I want. Anyway it's too late for that now.'

'But what about Pauline?' As he spoke, their daughter wandered into the sitting room, thumb in mouth. She hovered in the doorway.

'She'll be fine with me,' her mother said, smoothing Thelma's hair from her face as another contraction came. 'As soon as the midwife's here she can take over... then,' she said, winking at Pauline, 'we can see what a big girl you've become. Go and get me the Enid Blyton.'

'Come on, Son,' Thelma's father called from the hallway. He was already putting on his cap and making his way to the front door, the shrapnel in his leg making his limp pronounced. 'This is women's work – we'll leave them to it.'

Thelma smiled as she gazed around the room. 'The memories are all here, John. Mum, Dad, me and my brother Brian, your dad and Pauline… all growing up in this house.'

'I know, Nan. They were special times for all of you.'

'Their names are there… all there,' Thelma said pointing to the doorframe.

John looked at his grandmother for a moment, his head on one side, before gently taking her hand and leading her over to the doorway.

'What does this say, Nan?' he said pointing to the writing next to one of the marks on the frame.

Thelma placed her glasses on her nose and squinted at the letters. 'John. It says John age ten.'

'And this?' he said, pointing to one lower down.

'Jess and Tim age two.'

He indicated another.

'Jess and Tim age thirteen,' Thelma said, smiling at the thought of the twins. She hadn't seen as much of them as she'd have liked since the family had moved out of London.

'Memories are precious, Nan, but so are living people. We're on here too, remember. We all want to see more of you and it's difficult with you so far away in London. The Compulsory Purchase Order could be a blessing in disguise.'

'You may think so but it's not how it looks to me,' Thelma said. She picked up *Five on a Treasure Island* and handed it to her grandson. Her shoulders slumped. 'Here take this. I shan't be needing this at Green Acres.'

John raised his eyebrows. 'Who said anything about Green Acres, Nan? That's what Mum and Dad have been trying to speak to you about these last few weeks but you keep putting the phone down on them.'

Thelma felt a stab of guilt. It was true that she hadn't given her son the chance to speak when he rang and she had turned off the answer phone.

'We all want you to come and live with us. The new house has got an annex on the side. You could live there and still be independent. It would mean you'd get to see more of Jessie and Tim... and me of course.'

Thelma's eyes misted. 'You want me to live in Surrey with you?'

'That's if you want to. They're knocking the houses in your street down and there's nothing you or any of us can do to change that but you do get a choice where you live.' He ran his hand over the smooth cover of *Five on a Treasure Island* as generations of children had in their turn. 'It will be an adventure, Nan.'

Thelma ran her hand down the paintwork of the doorframe, now cream with age and etched with markings like the skin of a snake.

'What about this, John? My memories are all here.'

'Soon sort that out.' Thelma watched with wide eyes as her grandson went over to his toolbox and squatted down next to it. A few moments later, he sat back on his heels, a pleased look on his face. In his hands he held a screwdriver and a crowbar. He walked back to the doorframe.

'What are you doing?'

'Just what it looks like,' John said catching his lip between his teeth as he carefully inserted the screwdriver between the wall and the door trim. 'You should always take a memento with you from your old home, Nan... and this will do nicely.'

LIKE FATHER LIKE SON

If it hadn't have been for the bell on the door, Robert wouldn't even have noticed Mrs Lumley coming into the shop. As it was, the jingling, that always reminded him of Christmas, brought him sharply out of his thoughts.

'Penny for them, Robert.' Mrs Lumley manoeuvred her trolley bag in between the two display shelves of confectionary on which Robert had been stacking Snicker bars and Double Deckers.

He leant back on his heels and rubbed the small of his back. Replenishing the shelves was his least favourite job in his parent's newsagents but even this task gave him a certain amount of satisfaction – the way the sweet names conjured up images of his childhood.

Pick one, his father would say each Saturday morning after Robert had helped him fold the papers ready for the delivery boy. He would raise his eyes to the shelf and look at each plastic jar in turn, even though it was unnecessary, as he knew their contents by heart.

'I'm sorry, Mrs Lumley. I was day dreaming.'

'Some likely lass, I'll be bound.'

Robert blushed. 'No. It was nothing like that.'

Although Robert was eighteen, the closest he had come to kissing a girl was in a game of kiss chase at primary school when he had been pinned against the wall by a rather sturdy girl called Miriam.

'Can I help you with anything?'

'I was after your father actually. I've been having some problems with the wheel of my trolley bag and I wondered if he might take a look at it.'

'He's not here at the moment, Mrs Lumley. He's gone to the wholesalers. He'll be back before closing if you want to come back later.'

The elderly lady shook her head. 'No I don't think so. I won't want to be coming back out again. It takes me a while to get up the steps to my flat so I try and make sure that I do everything in one go.'

Robert straightened up. 'I could have a look at it for you, if you like.'

'Would you, dear? That would be most kind. I don't want you to be going to any trouble though.'

'It's no trouble, Mrs Lumley – take a seat and I'll give it the once over. Which wheel is it?' He pulled out the stool from behind the counter and helped her onto it.

'Your mum says you're off to university. Psychiatry did she say?'

Robert laughed. 'Psychology. It's the study of behaviour.'

'These newfangled ideas,' Mrs Lumley tutted. 'In my day boys went out to work at sixteen and earned a bit of money before settling down with a nice girl.'

Robert wanted to tell her that he rather liked that idea but instead he said, 'I think things have changed a bit since then, Mrs Lumley.'

'A lot of things have, Robert. My granddaughter took me to the new supermarket on the big roundabout last week. Service was dreadful – too busy to give you the time of day these checkout assistants. You should have seen how the girl raised her eyebrows when I couldn't get my purse out of my bag quick enough.'

'Well, I'm sorry to hear that.' Robert spun the trolley wheel and placed it back on the ground. 'Good as new. The axle was a bit bent, that was all. I've straightened it out for you.'

'You're a good boy, Robert,' Mrs Lumley said, taking his offered hand and stepping down from the stool. 'Just like your father. When are your exams?'

'I've taken two already. My English is next week but I help Dad out when I can't stand the sight of my revision books any more.'

He thought of the copy of *Anthony and Cleopatra* that lay open where he had left it on the kitchen table and felt his heart sink. The story didn't grab him and it was no surprise that at parents evening, his mum and dad had been told that this lack of interest was reflected in his course work. He was going to fail and let everyone down – he just knew it.

Robert watched his father frown as he studied the shop accounts at the kitchen table. He scratched his head and tapped out a rhythm on his front teeth with his pen. Even though he had been doing this for well over thirty years, Robert knew that it didn't come easily to him.

'I could take a look at that for you, Dad?' he said.

Greg looked at his son. 'Would you?'

Before he could answer, his mother turned from the stove. 'He'll do no such thing, Greg; he's got studying to do. The exams won't take themselves.'

Greg nodded. 'Your mother's right, Rob. You won't get to university if you don't get good grades. You don't want to end up a shop keeper like me.'

Robert's mother came up behind him and put her arms around his neck. 'We're so proud of you, Rob. Just think, the first one of our family to go to university. You've a chance to make something of yourself.'

Robert stared miserably at the book in front of him. *If only they knew*, he thought. *If only they knew.*

'So, I reckon that if I get the vet to clip his nails, it might stop him from ruining the new settee.' Mr West leaned his arms on the counter and straightened his cap.

'That's a good idea, Mr West. I was wondering how you were getting on with the new cat – you can never be sure of how they'll be if they've come from a rescue centre.'

'Oh, he's a good boy really. Company – especially in the evenings.'

'I imagine he is. How long's it been now?'

'Coming up to a year, lad. Still miss her though.'

'Course you do.' Robert shifted on the stool, reached over and picked up a copy of Cat World. 'Why don't you have a look in here? They've got good articles on all sorts of topics – I think you'd find it interesting.'

Mr West flicked through the pages. 'Think I might just do that, Robert. Good idea. How're the exams going? Your dad said that they're pinning their hopes on you – family honour and all that.'

Robert looked at the counter. 'I wish he wouldn't say that.'

'Have to say it will be strange not to see your face in the shop, though. Seems like only yesterday you were just a nipper following your dad around as he did the shelves.' Mr West laughed. 'I can still see you now, standing at the door and shaking everyone's hand as they came in. Gave me and Maud a right laugh.'

Robert remembered it too. He would puff out his chest and strut around the shop as if he owned it, memorising the names of the sweets and the newspapers. Then he would listen to his father chatting to the customers as they dawdled at the counter, watching him nod and smile and give words of advice. Wishing he could be him.

'You're a lot like your dad,' Mr West said, paying for the magazine and nodding to himself. 'A lot like him.'

The clock said twenty to ten. He had been in the exam for only forty minutes but he might as well have not gone in. He had filled half the page but he knew that there was nothing there that would constitute a good answer to the question: *What role do you think Enobarbus plays in the relationship between Antony and Cleopatra?*

Bizarrely his thoughts turned to the shop. The stocktaking was due and he knew that his father hated this job. He would give him a hand when he got back and see what he thought of the idea he had come up with to sell greetings cards alongside the papers and sweets.

Robert turned back to the paper and bent his head. *Enobarbus was Anthony's best friend and the voice of common sense,* he wrote. Then he drew a sharp line underneath, laid down his pen and walked out of the school hall.

'You're back early, Rob,' Greg said as Robert shoved open the shop door with his shoulder. Robert didn't answer but walked into the stockroom and found his grey overall. 'Thought the exam didn't finish until twelve.'

Robert sat heavily on the small stepladder they kept for reaching the higher shelves and put his head in his hands. The final exam was over but instead of relief he felt deflated: there would be nothing to celebrate. He hoped upon hope that his father wouldn't come into the dimly lit room.

There was silence for a moment and then Greg's voice again. 'I need to pop out for a bit. Do you mind keeping an eye on the shop till I get back?'

Robert took a deep breath. He could still see the look of surprise on his friends' faces as he left the hall. With an effort he pushed the memory away.

'That's fine, Dad. Take your time.'

He bent down and slit open the tape on the top of a box of Bounty bars with his penknife. He had meant to restock the shelf but instead, swung his leg over the stool behind the counter, unwrapped one of the bars and took a large bite from it.

Leaning his back against the cigarette stand, he breathed in deeply. The familiarity of the shop enveloped him with its smell of newsprint, assorted sweets and the burnt smell of the coffee his father liked to keep percolating in the back room. These were the smells of his childhood. They represented his hopes and dreams but he knew these were not the same dreams his parents held.

The shop bell made him jump. The girl standing in front of him hooked a sweep of dark hair behind her ear and put her head on one side.

'So this is the famous Robert who Gran can't stop talking about.'

Robert stopped chewing and quickly swallowed the half-chewed coconut. He wasn't sure how to respond and was glad when the girl helped him out.

'I'm Mrs Lumley's granddaughter, Jane.' She waited for this to register. 'Gran told me how you helped with her trolley the other day.'

'It was nothing,' Robert muttered. He felt suddenly tongue tied in the girl's presence.

'You'd be surprised at how much something like that means to an elderly person. You should have seen the staff at the new supermarket… not!'

'Yes, your grandmother told me.' Robert sat up straighter on the chair. 'I think it's sad really. Was there anything you wanted?'

'Not really. I just wanted to thank you for fixing Gran's trolley basket.' She started to go but something made Robert call out after her. 'Fancy a coffee? There's one made.'

Jane looked surprised but smiled and walked back. 'Never had coffee in a newsagents before.'

'Well we offer services above and beyond your usual selling of newspapers.'

'So I've heard,' Jane said. 'You'll be putting the Citizens Advice Bureau and The Samaritans out of business if you carry on like this.'

Robert laughed. She had certainly helped him to feel better and she really did have the most unusual violet eyes. He had just handed Jane her mug of coffee and was starting to tell her about his exam, when the door opened again and Mr West came in. In his hand he held a cat basket which he put on the counter. A pink nose could just be seen poking through the bars.

'Just had his nails clipped and was on my way home. Thought you might like to take a look at him.'

'Oh yes,' Robert said bending down and peering into the basket. 'He really is something isn't he?'

'Just bumped into Brian down the road from me, he mentioned the new whist evenings at the Community Centre that you told him about last week. Thought we might go along and see what's what.'

'Sounds a good idea, Mr West. I almost forgot…what did you make of Sunderland's two nil win last night?'

It was a while before Robert realised that Jane was trying to catch his eye. She mimed a drinking motion and when he nodded, disappeared into the back room, coming out again with a mug of coffee for the elderly man. In her other hand she held a second one.

'Gran will be here soon. I said I'd meet her in here. We don't want her to feel left out do we?'

Gradually the misery of the exam started to fade and Robert felt himself relax.

When he looked back on it, as his father was the only person who knew the secret of opening the shop door without the bell ringing, it was impossible to know how long he had been standing at the back of the shop. He had been showing a leaflet for the over 50's swimming session at the local pool to Brian, who had come in for his evening paper. Mr West had his cat out of the basket and it rubbed its white body against the chewing gum stand as Jane and her grandmother petted it.

'Sorry I was a bit longer than expected, Robert. I had a few things that I needed to sort out.'

Robert smiled. 'That's okay Dad. I can cope.' He looked at his watch. 'It's nearly closing anyway. I'll lock up if you like.'

He was unable to read his father's expression as he gave him a thumbs-up and tossed him the keys.

The smell of his favourite chicken casserole greeted him as he let himself into the flat above the shop. As he wondered what he was going to say to his mother about the exam, the feeling of calmness that had embraced him in the shop left him. His revision books were still on the kitchen table where he had left them the previous night. They sat there like an accusation and Robert made to pick them up.

'Leave them Rob. Just come and sit down for a moment. Your father and I want to talk to you.'

Robert's heart sank. This was it then. This would be the moment he let them down – when he would see the disappointment in their faces.

Greg came into the kitchen and placed the stock sheet in front of Robert. He opened the laptop. 'Thought we'd try the new accounting package you've been banging on about for the last twelve months. Want to show me how to use it?'

Robert was surprised. So they weren't going to ask him about the exam.

'Yeh, of course. It's really easy once you get the hang of it, Dad.' He pointed to the screen, his face lighting up. 'You just make a list of the stock here and add the amounts over in this column. Want to try?'

He stopped and looked at his father who was sitting quietly, studying his face.

'You enjoy this, don't you?' Greg said.

Robert hesitated. He felt that it was important how he answer his father's question. 'I like anything to do with the shop, Dad.'

Greg took off his glasses and rubbed his eyes. 'That's what Mr West told me when he came in this morning. Must have been about the time you were sitting your exam.'

Robert caught his breath. This was his mother's cue to ask how it had gone but instead she took off her apron and joined them at the table.

'I met Mrs Lumley in the High Street this morning. She told me how much they would all miss you if you go to university. She was with her granddaughter, Jane; you've met her, haven't you?' Robert had a fleeting vision of shiny black hair and violet eyes. 'She was telling me that she and a few of our locals have nominated you for the Community Award run by the local paper. You should be very proud of yourself.'

Proud? Robert could stand it no longer. 'I need to tell you both something.'

Greg closed the laptop and shook his head. 'Don't say anything Rob. We know. It was obvious something had gone wrong when you came back so early from your exam. I knew you wouldn't want to talk about it so I went to your school to find out what was going on.'

Robert hung his head. 'I'm sorry, Dad. I didn't know how to tell you. I just had a complete blank in the exam.'

'Mr Thomas said that as long as your other answers were fine, you might still be okay. The other exams went all right didn't they?'

Robert nodded and his father continued. 'You might still be able to get into Portsmouth but I don't think that's the point, do you?'

'What do you mean?' Robert said, looking from his father to his mother.

'The point is, Rob,' his mother said, taking his hand, 'that you don't want to go, do you? It's taken us a while to see what was under our noses. We realise now university wouldn't have made you happy. It was never your idea, was it? It was ours.'

Greg reached over to the dresser and picked up what looked like a brochure. He placed it in front of Robert. 'Mr Thomas gave me this. It's for Downbrook College. They apparently do a good basic accountancy course. Part time. They also do a business studies one. University's not for everyone – we see that now but doing one of the courses at the local college will help you in the future and it's all useful if you want to run a shop correctly.'

'You mean…?'

'I want you to join me in the shop on a permanent basis. The customers love you. You're an asset.'

'Just like *you* are, Greg.' Robert's mother kissed her husbands cheek. 'I remember the first day I met you. I'd come into the shop for a bag of sherbet dips and came out with an invitation to the local dance! Speaking of which.'

She rummaged in her handbag and pulled out a voucher for half price tickets to the film showing at the local cinema. She handed them to Robert. 'Jane was saying she's been wanting to see it for ages. I tore these out of the local paper. If I were you I'd see if she'd like you to take her – that's if you don't think I'm interfering again.'

Robert thought of Jane's violet eyes and gave his mother a wide grin. 'No, Mum. I'll ask her.' He made his face serious. 'It will be my way of helping the community.'

'And as we know you're very good at that,' his mother laughed, putting her arm around her two boys. 'Like father like son!'

THE LAST ROSE

'I wouldn't ask, Catherine. Only I feel that if I don't go now, I probably never shall.'

Ron is standing in my doorway and the look on his face tells me that he's been worried about asking.

I wave him into the kitchen. 'Why would I mind? It's only a bit of watering and pruning, after all.'

'I know that. It's just that I always seem to be asking you for favours. It was the cake for the church bring and buy sale last week and feeding the cat when I went to Bournemouth with the bowls club the week before.'

I set a cup of Earl Grey in front of him and study his face. 'Look, Ron. I'm just glad that you're out and about again. It's what Glad would have wanted.'

Ron stirs a spoonful of sugar into his tea. 'When you lose someone, you think that you'll never get over it, don't you?'

I nod, remembering the dark days after Dennis died. 'And when everyone says that time will help, you feel so angry. I remember wanting to shout out, *But how do you know?*'

Ron laughs. 'I remember you telling me that at the time, Cath. I can't tell you how much it helped... knowing that I wasn't the only one to feel like that.'

We sit for a while, lost in our own thoughts.

'Anyway,' Ron's voice sounds apologetic, the way it always does when he's asking me a favour. 'If you're sure you don't mind.'

I pat his hand. 'I know you'd do the same for me. What are neighbours for, if we can't be asked a few favours every now and again? You go off and have a lovely time at Jane's. It will be great for the children to see their grandfather. You ought to go more often, Ron.'

'I'd love to but you know how I hate to leave the garden. It was Glad's pride and joy, as you know, and I sort of made a promise to myself to look after it just as she would – even though she used to say I didn't know one end of a garden fork from the other.'

I chuckle, remembering how Glad had told me, over a cup of tea, how Ron had once dug up her sunflowers, thinking they were weeds. 'I'm sure you do your best with the garden and Glad would be very proud of you for it.'

'Do you think so?'

'I know so. Anyway...' I take my diary out of my handbag. 'You say you'll be away from the second for five days. Let me see... that takes us to the seventh. Do you want me to walk around the garden with you so you can show me what you want doing?'

'Well, if it's not too much trouble.'

'None at all, Ron. We'll finish our tea and then we can take a look.'

Ron's garden is bigger than mine, even though we live on the same street. Beyond the lawn, a gravel path leads down through wide borders. They are a riot of early summer colour. I stop and look at the flowers: purple heads of alliums compete with pink pelargoniums and the yellow spikes of lupins and in between, clouds of white and pink baby's breath and delicate forget-me-nots fill the gaps.

Ron sees me looking. 'As you can see, I don't really know what I'm doing. Glad used to have it all worked out in her head. She knew what was tall and what was short and everything was in its right place. It's not exactly what she would have had in mind.'

'Well, I think it's marvellous,' I say, and I mean it. The borders remind me of an impressionist painting, the shapes and colours vying with each other for attention. 'It reminds me of one of those Kaleidoscopes I had as a child.'

Ron smiles. 'I'm glad you think so, Cath. That means a lot to me.'

But it isn't the borders that make me catch my breath. The path takes us to an opening in a hedge and Ron stands back and holds out his arm to let me through. In the small area beyond is a little rose garden. In the beds, tea roses are blooming: blush pink, ruby red, and the palest yellow. How strange that in all the years I have known Ron, I have never walked around his garden.

The path leads down the centre of the beds to where a little stone bench sits beneath a black metal arbour. When I bend to sit, the stone is warm beneath my skirt where the sun has bathed it. I breathe deeply, filling my nose with the roses' delicate fragrance.

'If you wouldn't mind giving them a good soaking while I'm away and just tie in any loose ends, I'd be very grateful.'

I think of what a pleasure it will be to walk in Ron's beautiful garden each evening when the air is still and the heady scent of the flowers is at their peak.

I reach out my hand to the arbour. An old, established rose climbs the trellis and from its twisted branches hang faded blooms of an exquisite pale apricot.

'Beautiful, isn't it. It was Glad's favourite – an early flowerer. It's had its best show, though. It'll be over soon.'

'Not quite,' I say, touching a fat green bud, just splitting and showing its apricot underskirts to the world. 'Here is the last rose... and the last one is often the most precious for being so.'

Ron sits down next to me. 'Glad must have thought the same thing. Ordinarily, she didn't like to cut the roses, preferred to see them growing in the garden, but she used to pick the last rose from this climber and make me wear it in my buttonhole.'

'Very dapper you must have looked too. Well, this last rose should be perfect for your return, Ron. I'll make sure I look after it for you.'

'I know you will, Cath,' Ron says, patting my arm. 'You're very good at looking after.'

Ron has been gone four days and each morning and evening I have fed the cat and picked up the post, then finally, with a watering can filled from the outside tap, have made my way down the gravel path to the rose garden. After watering the roses, I sit on the stone seat and watch the petals collecting on the path beneath the arbour then look to see how the last bloom is progressing.

The day after Ron had left, the rose had finally peeled away its green sepals to reveal a rich orange bud. Two days later, its petals had unfurled into a whorl of velvet petals of the most delicate apricot imaginable. If only I had tied the stem in while I had thought about it, but the air that evening was still with only the hint of the heaviness that precedes a storm.

Now, I dodge the puddles on the uneven path and tie my rain hood tighter around my head. This time, I don't have my watering can, as the rain will have done the job for me during the night, but with Ron arriving home later this morning, I want to make sure that the last rose has survived the night's storm.

As I walk through the gap in the hedge, I can see, almost immediately, the damage the wind and the rain have caused. A carpet of soggy, pastel-coloured petals, brown around the edges, cover the beds and stick to the paths. I walk to the arbour but I can see, even before I reach the bench, that the last rose is no longer there – snapped from its stem by the thieving winds.

How ridiculous, to feel sad over a flower but the truth is, I wanted to see Ron's face when he saw it. Wanted to know he was happy.

'What's the sad face for?'

Spinning round, I see Ron standing in the gap in the hedge. 'Ron! I wasn't expecting you back until later.'

'I came home last night. Thought I'd best drive back before the storm. I didn't want to bother you so late and knew I'd catch you this morning. You've done a grand job, Catherine. I am very grateful to you.'

'But I haven't Ron, that's the whole point.' I survey the rose garden and feel an inexplicable wave of sadness. 'You see, the last rose has gone. You never saw it.'

'No, Cath, that's where you're wrong.' He walks towards me and in his hand is the rose, its creamy, apricot petals curling inwards from his palm, as beautiful as I have ever seen it. He holds it out as one might a precious gift. 'I cut it when I got home.'

'For me?'

'Yes, the last rose is for you, Catherine.' Ron threads the rose through the lapel of my jacket and then stands for a moment, his hands on my shoulders. 'My very dear friend.'

ABOUT THE AUTHOR

Wendy Clarke lives in Sussex with her husband, cat and step-dog. She writes short fiction and articles for national magazines. You can find out more about Wendy on her blog:

http://wendyswritingnow.blogspot.co.uk

If you have enjoyed reading this collection of short stories, please consider leaving a review on Amazon.

Another book by Wendy Clarke that you may enjoy:

Room in Your Heart – A collection of romantic stories

She kept a special room in her heart. For a while, the door was locked and then, one day, she felt able to visit the room and realised that, instead of being a place to fear, it was full of happiness...

Room in Your Heart, is a collection of twelve romantic short stories of love and loss, previously published in The People's Friend Magazine. If you like stories with emotional depth and a satisfying ending then these stories will not fail to leave you unmoved.

Printed in Great Britain
by Amazon